BEAMS OF FIRE

Slocum rode at the head of Tipton's cowhands right onto the Beamer spread and up to the house. Maw Beamer came out onto the porch with her shotgun.

"What do you want here?" she demanded.

"We came for Hump and Brace Beamer," said Slocum. "They're both wanted by the law."

"They ain't here. And the first one of you that gets off his horse is going to get a belly full of shot."

Slocum turned his big Appaloosa and started riding away from the house. The other riders followed him. When they were beyond the shotgun's range, they all dismounted and found cover. A rifle at one window started firing, and Slocum's men returned fire.

Maw went out the back door with her rifle and edged up to a corner of the house to peer around. She caught sight of a cowboy lurking behind a barrel, took aim, and fired. The cowboy yelped and fell to the ground.

"Behind the house," Slocum shouted, and fired a barrage of shots. Maw shrieked, hit in the shoulder. She dropped the rifle, and another shot hit her in the chest. Inside the house, Henley Beamer took a bullet through the side of his head. About that same time, Hiram Beamer was hit. By then Randy had walked around the house on the outside.

"Hey, Slocum," Randy said.

"What is it?" Slocum walked toward the corner of the house where Randy waited, and he saw the body of the old woman.

"I guess we killed her," said Randy.

"Not before she killed one of our boys, ..ocum said. "It's pretty clear where these Beamers got their dispositions."

JAKE LOGAN

SLOCUM

AND THE BAD-NEWS
BROTHERS

JOVE BOOKS, NEW YORK

SLOCUM AND THE BAD-NEWS BROTHERS

A Jove Book / published by arrangement with
the author

PRINTING HISTORY
Jove edition / April 2004

ISBN: 0-515-13715-4

A JOVE BOOK®
Jove Books are published by The Berkley Publishing Group,
a division of Penguin Group (USA) Inc.,
375 Hudson Street, New York, New York 10014.
JOVE and the "J" design
are trademarks belonging to Penguin Group (USA) Inc.

PRINTED IN THE UNITED STATES OF AMERICA

10 9 8 7 6 5 4 3 2 1

1

Slocum sat alone in the Hogneck Saloon in the small town of Breakneck in some far-flung, godforsaken place. He was nursing a bottle of brown whiskey, three fingers at a time poured into a small glass. He wondered what the hell he was doing in this damn place anyway. He'd had a job back in Texas, but there had been some trouble. He'd decided it was time to move on, and so he had moved. He hadn't paid much attention to the direction of his travels, and somehow he had wound up in Breakneck. There wasn't much to it. One main street with few buildings. One served as hotel, saloon, general store, and whorehouse. He hadn't paid any mind to the others, except for the stable where he had boarded his Appaloosa before heading into the Hogneck to drown his memories or his miseries or something.

The whiskey was good, but he had paid dearly for the bottle. He was wondering how much a meal would cost and how good it would be. He decided that it would sure as hell beat his own trail cooking, and he waved at the barkeep. The man sauntered over to his table. He didn't have very many customers in the place anyhow. "Want something?" he asked.

"Can I get a meal in here?" Slocum asked.

"Steak and eggs and taters," the man said.

"It got bread with it?"

"It can."

"I want some bread with it."

"Be a few minutes," the man said, and he turned and ambled back behind the bar and went through a door there into a back room. Slocum guessed it was the kitchen. He was a little put off by the man's appearance, and he had hoped that there was someone else back there. The man was sloppy and wearing dirty clothes. Apparently he was the cook as well as the bartender. Oh, well, Slocum would try not to think about it. He lifted his glass for another drink. At least the whiskey was good. Just then the front door was opened, and Slocum felt a blast of cold wind as a cowboy stepped in and shut the door behind himself. The cowboy shook the cold off his frame and then looked behind the bar. He turned his head toward Slocum.

"Where's Goosey?" he asked.

Slocum shrugged. "I don't know anyone by that name," he said.

"The bartender," the cowboy explained.

"Oh. Well, I guess it's my fault he ain't here. I ordered up a meal, and he went back to cook it."

"Well, hell, I want a drink."

"Grab a glass and come on over. I'll buy you a drink, since it's my fault the barkeep is out of the room."

The cowboy looked at Slocum and at the bottle on Slocum's table. "All right," he said. He turned to the bar and picked up a glass. He looked at it closely, decided that it was clean, and walked over to the table where Slocum was seated. Sticking out his right hand toward Slocum, he said, "I'm Randy Self."

Slocum shook the hand. "Slocum," he said. "Sit down."

Self pulled out a chair and sat. He put his glass on the table, and Slocum poured him a drink. "Thanks," said Self. He lifted the glass and took a swallow. "Whew. You got the good stuff there all right."

"Whiskey's one thing a man ought not to be cheap about," said Slocum.

"Well, I won't argue with that."

"You work around here, do you?" Slocum asked.

"Out on the Tipton place," Self said. "What about you?"

"Just passing through."

Self laughed. "That's a good one," he said.

"What do you mean?"

"Hell, I didn't think that Breakneck was on the way to anyplace from anyplace else. I never thought it could be just passed through. Figured a man would have to head for it deliberately to get here."

"You're probably mostly right about that. I just kind of blundered into it, I guess. I rode out of Texas not headed for anyplace in particular, and here I am."

"You said that right. You're right here in no place in particular."

Goosey came back just then bringing Slocum's meal. He dropped it on the table in front of Slocum, and Slocum paid for it. He looked at it carefully. It seemed to be edible. He cut off a piece of the steak and popped it in his mouth and started chewing. After he swallowed, he said, "It'll do." Self finished his drink and started to get up, but Slocum refilled his glass. Then he went on eating.

"Thanks," Self said. "So you come from Texas. You work on a cow outfit there?"

"Um-hum," muttered Slocum

"The law chase you out?"

Slocum looked up at Self, and Self smiled. "Hey," he said, "I was just funning."

Slocum swallowed hard. "You might say I was chased out," he said.

"Well, hell, I been chased out of a couple of places in my time," said Self. "I guess that's how come I've stuck around Breakneck so long. I ain't got myself in no trouble here, so no one's tried to chase me out."

Slocum finished his meal and put the dirty plate on the table behind him. He picked up his glass and drained it. Then he poured it full again. He looked over at Self and saw that his glass was getting low. He held the bottle out and Self shoved his glass toward Slocum. Slocum poured it full.

"Thanks again, pard," Self said. "I sure am drinking up a share of your good whiskey."

"It's all right," Slocum said. "It's paid for, and I ain't

had no one to talk to except my horse for some time now."

"You wouldn't be looking for a job, would you?"

"I ain't been real active about it," said Slocum, "but if one was to pop up in front of me, I might be interested."

"I might could get you on out to Tipton's."

Slocum shrugged. Four men came through the front door and walked up to the bar.

"The place'll start to get busy now," Self said. "It's about time."

As if to back him up, three more men came walking in. Then three tired-looking girls came down the stairs. One of them made for the table where Slocum and Self were seated. The other two headed for the two other groups of men. The first of the girls sat down beside Slocum. "Howdy, stranger," she said.

"Howdy," said Slocum. "I ain't unfriendly. I'll buy you a drink if you like, but that's all."

"Oh."

"I can't speak for this other feller though."

She got up and moved over next to Self. "Do you like girls?" she asked him. "Or are you like your friend here?"

Slocum rankled a bit. He thought about telling the whore that he liked girls all right. He just wasn't very fond of tired-looking whores. He didn't. He kept his mouth shut. The girl waved at Goosey, and Goosey brought her a glass. Slocum poured some whiskey in it. She picked it up and took a sip. Then she took the hat off Self's head and tousled his hair. Self grinned.

"I'm real friendly, honey," he said.

She nibbled on his ear and whispered in it, and the two of them finished their drinks and got up from the table. Self gave Slocum a look as he walked with the girl toward the stairway. Slocum tipped his hat and watched them go. The door opened and two more men walked in. One of them was wearing an expensive suit, boots, and hat. He was a big man, robust, clean shaven. Slocum figured him to be around sixty years old, and he noticed that the man was not wearing a gun. The man with him was a bit younger and dressed as a working cowhand. He was armed.

Slocum poured himself another drink. He wasn't paying attention to what was going on around him in the saloon. He was thinking about Randy Self's offer of asking about a job for him. He wondered if he really wanted to hang around this place. It sure wasn't much of a town. The ranch might be something else though. You could never tell. Maybe, he thought, he'd wait till Randy had asked. If he was offered the job, he could look over the ranch and see what he thought about it. He wasn't broke, but his money wouldn't last him forever. He could work here for a spell, save up a little more money, and then head out again if he didn't like it. He decided that was what he would do. He glanced over at the stairway and saw Randy and the girl coming back down. He was about to look away when he saw the expression on the young cowboy's face change.

"Hey! Look out!" Randy shouted.

Slocum looked toward where Randy's eyes were trained, and he saw a man with a gun in his hand aimed at the back of the unarmed man in the suit. He could see that the man had just pulled back the hammer. At Randy's warning, everyone looked around. The man in the suit did not panic.

"Beamer," he said, "you can see that I'm not armed."

"I don't give a shit," said the man called Beamer. "I'm going to kill you."

The cowboy who was with the man in the suit looked as if he wanted to go for his gun, but Beamer shifted his aim over to cover him. "Don't try it," he said. "I'll kill you, too."

It was a touchy situation, and clearly it was none of Slocum's business. He didn't really want to kill someone in this town anyway. Even so, he hated sitting idly by and watching a cold-blooded murder, and the man in the suit was unarmed. Slowly, he reached out with his right hand and grabbed the neck of his bottle. Then as quickly as he could move, he stood up, cocked the bottle over his shoulder, and heaved it with all his might. As it hurtled through the air, it slung whiskey all along its path. Then it crashed into the side of Beamer's head. He had not seen it coming, and he dropped like a sack of grain. The cowhand with the man in the suit ran over and picked up Beamer's gun. He took it to Goosey and tossed it on the bar.

"Put this away," he said.

The man in the suit walked toward Slocum. He reached the table at the same time as Randy Self.

"That was a hell of a toss," Randy said.

"I owe you," said the man in the suit, reaching forward with his right hand.

"That's all right," said Slocum, shaking the hand. "I like to see a man get a fair shake."

"Say, Slocum," said Randy, "this here is my boss."

"Oh, yeah?" Slocum said.

"Hell, yeah. You just saved the life of Mr. Tipton."

"And your name is Slocum?" said Tipton.

"That's right."

"How do you know Randy?"

"I don't really," Slocum said. "I just bought him a drink tonight."

Over Tipton's shoulder, Slocum could see someone coming in the door with a star on his vest. He was a little surprised to find that Breakneck had a lawman. The lawman directed a couple of men to lift Beamer and drag him out of the saloon. Slocum figured that the bastard was being taken to jail. Randy started to say something more to Tipton, but he saw that the lawman was walking toward them so he held his tongue.

"Carl," said the lawman.

Tipton turned around to face him.

"Tell me what happened here, Carl."

"Beamer came up behind me with a gun in his hand. He aimed it at me and cocked it and said that he was going to kill me. Mr. Slocum here tossed a bottle and decked him."

The lawman looked at Slocum. "Slocum is it?" he said.

"It is," said Slocum.

"That what happened?"

"Yeah."

"How come you did it?"

"I don't like watching a murder done," said Slocum.

"That all?"

"What else could there be?"

The lawman shrugged. "I can't think of anything. You're a stranger here."

It was not a question, so Slocum did not give it an answer. The sheriff extended his hand. "I'm Seth Willis, the sheriff here. We appreciate what you did."

Slocum shook the sheriff's hand. "All it cost me was half a bottle of whiskey," he said.

Tipton waved at Goosey. "Bring a bottle of your best bourbon," he called out. "Shall we sit down?"

"I better be getting back," said Willis. "Thanks just the same. Slocum, thanks again."

Slocum touched the brim of his hat as Willis turned to leave. Then he sat down and so did Randy and Tipton. Tipton then hailed the cowhand who had come in with him, and the man walked over.

"Sit down, Lige," said Tipton. Then he turned to Slocum. "Do you mind?"

"No."

"Mr. Slocum, this is Lige Phillips. He's my foreman."

"Glad to meet you," Lige said, shaking Slocum's hand across the table. "That was sure quick thinking, Mr. Slocum."

"Let me get one thing straight here," Slocum said. "I ain't no mister. Just Slocum will do."

"It was quick thinking," said Tipton, "and a damn good aim, too."

Goosey brought a bottle and some more glasses, and Tipton poured drinks all around. Slocum raised his glass. "Thanks," he said.

"It's the least I could do," said Tipton.

They all sipped at their whiskey. Then Randy said, "Mr. Tipton?"

"Yes?"

"Earlier this evening, before you come in, I told Slocum here that I'd ask if you had any jobs open."

"Are you looking for work, Slocum?" Tipton asked.

"I am kind of footloose just now," Slocum said.

"I can tell by your look that you're a cow man," said

Tipton. "If you want work, you've got a place with me."

"Thank you," said Slocum. "I'd like to look the place over first."

"That's a good answer," said Tipton. "What do you say to riding out with us tonight? You can stay the night as my guest and look things over in the morning."

"All right."

They had another round of drinks and decided to leave. Slocum corked the bottle and handed it to Tipton. "It's yours," said Tipton. Slocum took the bottle as they left the Hogneck. Tipton, Phillips, and Randy headed for their horses at the hitch rail, and Tipton looked at Slocum. "You have a horse?" he asked.

"He's in the stable," Slocum said. "I'll fetch him and meet you back here."

The other three men climbed into their saddles. Lige Phillips watched Slocum walk toward the stable. "Mr. Tipton," he said, "I don't like to interfere."

"What is it, Lige?"

"That Slocum, he done you a good turn. That's for sure."

"But?"

"He sure has the look of a gunfighter to me."

2

The four men passed around what was left of the bottle of bourbon on their ride out to the Tipton spread, so by the time they arrived, they were pretty well soused. They stopped in front of the porch of Tipton's big house. Lige Phillips said, "Mr. Tipton, me and Randy here'll take care of your horse, and we'll get ole Slocum here bedded down, too."

"Take his horse and mine," Tipton said. "Slocum's my guest tonight. We'll get him settled in tomorrow if he's a mind to stay on."

"Yes sir," said Phillips. Even in his semi-stupor, Slocum thought that he detected a look of—what? Jealousy? Suspicion?

"Good night," said Randy Self.

Tipton swung down out of his saddle and staggered a bit as Phillips grabbed the reins. Slocum dismounted, too, and handed his reins to Self. "Thanks, Randy," he said. Tipton started up the steps to the porch. He stumbled once and grabbed the rail to right himself.

"Come on, Slocum," he said.

Slocum followed the ranch owner up to the front door where Tipton fumbled with the handle a bit before he managed to get the door opened. Then he swung it wide, staggered back a couple of steps. At last he walked through the door and Slocum followed. Inside he turned and shut the door.

"Carl, is that you?" came a female voice.

"It's me," Tipton called out. "I've got company. Don't bother getting up. I'll take care of everything."

"Are you sure?"

"I'm sure. Go back to sleep."

Tipton weaved his way over to a liquor cabinet and grabbed a bottle by the neck. He picked up a couple of glasses and made his way over to a small table that stood in front of a couple of stuffed chairs. Putting the glasses down on the table, he poured them full of whiskey and gestured toward Slocum. "Thanks," said Slocum, reaching for one of the glasses. Tipton put the bottle down heavily and dropped onto one of the chairs. He pointed at the other chair, and Slocum sat down.

"I ain't ready to call it a day," he said. "How about you?"

"I'm just going along with you, Mr. Tipton," Slocum said. "This hits the spot all right."

"Call me Carl," Tipton said. "Hell, Slocum, you saved my life tonight. I don't take that lightly."

Slocum shrugged, but before he could say anything, Tipton started in again. "You done it slick as hell, too," he said. "I don't believe I ever saw anything like it."

"That ole boy's likely to come after you again when he sobers up and gets out of jail," Slocum said.

"Hell, he's liable to come after you, too, after what you done to him."

"I don't think he even saw me," said Slocum.

"Maybe not, but someone'll tell him who done it. If you don't want trouble with him, maybe you'd ought to light on out of here first thing in the morning."

"I can handle myself," Slocum said. "Besides, I don't think he'll be out of jail that quick."

"Yeah," said Tipton, looking sideways at Slocum. "I imagine you can handle yourself all right. Lige said you got the look of a gunfighter."

Slocum looked at Tipton and started to open his mouth.

"That's all right," Tipton said. "I don't mind."

"I can punch cows, too," Slocum said.

"Yeah. I can tell that. I said that earlier, didn't I?"

"Yes sir. You did."

"Slocum, I've got an extra bedroom here in the house. It's a back room, and it's got its own door for coming and going. I want you to work for me, but I don't want another cowboy. I want a bodyguard. I want you to go where I go. Stick close. That Beamer, the man you conked tonight, he'll be back after me. And even if he don't get me, he's got five brothers and four cousins or something like that on a ranch near here. They all stick together. I don't fancy sitting still here on the ranch. I'll pay you ten dollars more a month than I pay for cowboy wages. You'll take your meals here in the house with us. What do you say?"

"I don't know," Slocum said. "I was thinking about a puncher's job. I wasn't looking to hire on as a gunfighter."

"You can think on it overnight if you've a mind to."

"What have these Beamers got against you?"

"It goes back a ways," Tipton said. "I took some money away from one of them in a poker game at the Hogneck one time. He accused me of cheating, but he didn't do nothing about it. Didn't have the guts while I was looking at him. A while later I caught one of his brothers fixing to use a running iron on one of my cows. I roped him and dragged him a ways into the stream and left him there. Run his horse off. It was a kind of cold day, and he had a long walk. I guess he took it kind of personal."

"Seems kind of small-minded," Slocum said. He tipped his glass back and finished his drink. Tipton refilled it. "But I reckon there are folks who think like that."

"Well, what do you say?"

"Let me give you an answer in the morning when I'm sober," Slocum said. "Hell, I might agree to fight a damned grizzly bear tonight."

"That's fair enough."

"Hell, when you sober up, you might not want me around anyhow."

Tipton laughed. He tried to stand up, but he didn't quite make it. Slocum stood up and gave him a hand. Tipton came to his feet with a lurch, nearly falling over forward. Both men laughed at that. Then Tipton managed to show Slocum the extra room and get himself to bed.

Slocum woke up a little later than his usual time, but it still was not too late. He got up and dressed. There was a washbasin and a pitcher of water on a table by the wall, and he made use of those. Then he went out the back door to find the outhouse. In a short while, he walked around the house to the front porch, found a chair, and sat down. He took out a cigar and lit it with a match. He was puffing contentedly when the door opened and Tipton stepped out.

"There you are," he said.

"I made use of the back door," Slocum said. "I didn't want to startle the lady of the house."

"Well, stay right there," Tipton said. "I'll bring us out some coffee."

He went back inside, and Slocum continued to smoke. Tipton was back in a jiffy with two cups of coffee. He gave one to Slocum and pulled himself up a chair.

"How's your head this morning?" he said.

"I'm doing fine," Slocum said. "It was good whiskey."

"You sound like a man who knows how to drink."

"Well, I've done it aplenty."

"Breakfast is fixing," Tipton said. "It ought to be about ready by the time you finish that cigar."

"Sounds good," Slocum said. "I'm kind of tired of my own cooking."

Lige Phillips came riding up to the porch just then. He touched the brim of his hat and nodded at Slocum. "Mr. Tipton," he said, "I'm sending a half dozen boys up to the north pasture to look for strays and three boys down south to mend that fence. You want me to take Slocum and get him set up?"

"Me and Slocum are still dickering, Lige. Go ahead and do what you said. That sounds good to me."

"Okay," Lige said. "Slocum," he said, nodding his head as he turned his horse to ride on.

"Lige is a good man," Tipton said.

"He seems to feel a little cautious toward me," said Slocum. "That's probably good."

"He's protective all right," Tipton said. "Of me personally and of my cattle and my money."

"Then what do you need me for?"

"Lige is protective all right," Tipton said, "but he's no gunfighter. Even if he was, he's busy running this ranch for me. I can't go calling on him every time I want to ride into town or go visit a neighbor ranch or something like that."

Slocum nodded. He took a final puff on his cigar and tossed the stub away. Tipton stood up. "Let's go in," he said. They took their cups and went into the house where Slocum was astonished to see two women setting the table. One he took to be Tipton's wife. She was a good-looking woman. He guessed her to be in her fifties, a little younger than her husband, and she was well taken care of. She looked around and smiled as the two men walked in. The other was younger. She could have been anywhere from twenty-five to thirty. And she was a knockout. She was dressed in jeans and a shirt, and they showed off her figure to perfection. Her hair was long and light brown, almost blonde. She headed back into the kitchen when the men walked in, and Slocum couldn't help but watch the sway of her hips as she moved.

"Myrtle," said Tipton to the older woman, "I want you to meet Slocum. Slocum, this here is my wife, Myrtle."

Slocum took off his hat. "It's a pleasure, ma'am," he said.

Just then the younger woman came back into the room carrying a bowl which she placed on the table. "And this is Jamie," Tipton said. "Our daughter. Jamie, say hello to Slocum."

"Just Slocum?" said Jamie.

"My first name's John," said Slocum, "but I hardly ever use it."

"All right then, Slocum," said Jamie. "Pleased to meet you. Have a seat." She gestured toward a chair, and Slocum pulled it out from the table and sat down. Tipton sat in his chair. Myrtle brought the coffeepot and refilled the cups, and in another moment the ladies were also seated. On the table was a platter of fried eggs, a platter of slices of ham, a bowl of potatoes, a bowl of gravy, a bowl of beans, and a bowl of biscuits. Tipton helped himself and passed the dishes on to Slocum.

"So what brings you to these parts, Slocum?" Jamie asked.

"I was just passing through," Slocum said. "I met your father last night."

"In the Hogneck," said Tipton. "Me and Lige had just bellied up to the bar, when that damn Brace Beamer drew down on me from behind. He threatened to kill me, and Slocum swung a bottle and beaned him on the noggin. Knocked him clean out. It was the damndest shot I've ever seen."

"It sounds like we all owe you thanks," Myrtle said.

"This meal is thanks enough," Slocum said. "It's as good as I've ever had."

"Thank you," said Myrtle.

"Glad you like it," Jamie said. "Eat all you want."

"I've offered Slocum a job," said Tipton. "Bodyguarding me. He's thinking on it."

"What will you do, Slocum?" Jamie asked. "Carry bottles around with you to throw at anyone who threatens Daddy?"

Slocum grinned. "That might not be a bad idea," he said. "It did work last night."

"He's wearing a Colt that I bet you he can handle just fine," said Tipton, a little aggravation in his voice.

"I'm sure he can," said Myrtle.

When they were all done with their meal, Myrtle refilled the coffee cups for Slocum and Tipton, and she and Jamie started clearing the table. "Let's go back out on the porch," Tipton said. He took his cup and headed for the front door. Slocum followed. Soon they were seated again out on the porch. "Have you thought over my offer yet?" Tipton asked.

"Is there anything you ain't told me about?" Slocum asked.

"Like what?"

"Anything. Rustlers. A range war. Anything."

"Nothing. Not a damn thing. Just them goddamned Beamer bastards. Brace was ready to shoot me in the back last night. I been expecting something like that, but that was the first time. I figure after what happened last night in the Hogneck, they'll all be after me now. No. I ain't got no other trouble. Nothing I know about anyways. I always tried to get along with my neighbors. And I've always done a good job of it. Till the Beamers."

"So just what do I do? Act like your shadow?"

"When I'm around the house here, you can do whatever you want. I just want you to be ready to ride out with me whenever I go anywhere off the ranch. None of them Beamers got the guts to come onto the ranch."

"So if you're not going anywhere, all I do is lay around here on my ass and draw top wages?"

"That's about it."

"It don't seem hardly fair," said Slocum. "It's liable to make for some hard feelings among the cowhands. Especially that Lige."

"You let me worry about my crew," Tipton said. "Ole Lige will go along with anything I tell him to, whether he likes it or not."

"I'd feel better about it," Slocum said, "if on the days when you don't need me to ride out with you, you'd let me work along with the rest of the boys."

"That's up to you. I said you can do whatever the hell you want to do when I'm just hanging around here. If you want to work, hell, go on ahead and work. Well, what do you say?"

Slocum looked out and around. The ranch looked good. He got along fine so far with old Tipton and with Myrtle. Jamie was something else. He thought that he'd like a chance to get along better with her, but then, that might be the way to get into some real trouble. He knew Randy and Lige, and they were both all right. Randy was a good kid. Lige was suspicious of Slocum, and he could be a problem. He might easily get jealous of Slocum's position of privilege. But then, Tipton had said that he would handle that. There was no telling about the others. He would just have to find out.

"Well, Carl," he said, "let's give it a try."

Tipton stood up with a wide grin across his face and reached out his right hand to pump Slocum's. "All right," he said. "Good. You're on the payroll starting right now. Good."

"Can I meet the rest of the hands?"

"We can get started," Tipton said. "Some of them's already out working. But we'll get started."

He moved to the front door and jerked it open. "Myrtle," he called out. "Jamie. Slocum's staying with us." He turned away from the door and started down the stairs. "Come on, Slocum. Let's walk out to the corral."

It wasn't a long walk, and they found Lige there with two more cowhands. They looked up when they saw their boss coming.

"Lige," Tipton said, "Slocum's on the payroll. Boys, meet Slocum. These are Ace and Trotter."

Slocum shook hands with the two cowhands. They had apparently gotten their instructions from Lige, and so they excused themselves and went to catch a couple of horses. When Lige was alone, Tipton told him about the job he had given Slocum. Lige did not look happy about it.

"Lige," said Slocum, "I'd like to pull my weight around here. I can do ranch work. If Carl ain't needing me, I'd like to work like any other cowhand."

Lige looked at Slocum suspiciously. Then he looked at Tipton.

"You need him today?" he asked.

"I'll just be hanging around the house today," Tipton said. "He's free to do whatever he wants to do."

"All right, Slocum," Lige said. "I'll put your ass to work."

3

Slocum wasn't at all prepared for what happened next. Lige rode out with him to show him a section of fence that needed to be repaired and left him to do the work. Slocum didn't grumble. He set right to it. But when Lige had ridden away, he'd said out loud, "Son of a bitch." He had thought that he might be out riding herd somewhere, but he should have known that the dirty bastard would put him to the worst jobs he could find. He knew that Lige did not like him. The foreman would much rather Old Man Tipton had not hired him on in the first place. He had Slocum pegged as a gunfighter, and so he had no use for him. He would like to see Slocum just ride on.

But Slocum thought, I brought it on myself. I said I could work, and I wanted to work rather than lay around the house. So he worked. He worked hard till noon when Lige came riding back up and said it was time to go back for chow. Slocum mounted up and rode along with Lige back to the main house. He started to go along with him to the cookshack, but Lige scowled and said, "The boss says that you're taking your meals in the big house." Slocum dismounted there in front of the main ranch house and went on inside. Tipton met him at the door.

"Slocum," he said, a broad smile on his face, "come on in. Lunch is about ready."

"Thank you," Slocum said, taking off his hat and hanging it on the tree that stood by the front door. Just then, Myrtle came out of the kitchen with a bowl in her hands.

She saw Slocum and greeted him with a smile. Slocum nodded. Myrtle put the bowl on the table and went back into the kitchen. A moment later Jamie appeared with a platter of steaks. "How do you do, ma'am?" Slocum said.

"Oh, much better now that you're here," she said, but she said it with an edge to her voice that indicated more than a touch of sarcasm. Slocum smiled. He guessed that he had let himself in for quite a bit of that when he had taken Tipton's offer.

"Have a chair," said Tipton. "My brother's coming by to eat with us. I want you to meet him."

"Your brother?" said Slocum.

"Yeah. He's got a small spread north of here. We don't get together very often. He sent a man over with a note saying that he was coming by, so we set him an extra place."

"I'd be happy to eat with the boys," Slocum said. "I don't want to be in the way here."

"Nonsense," said Tipton. "When I hired you on, I said you'd eat in the house. And like I just said, I want you to meet Arnie. Arnie, that's my brother. He ought to be getting here any time now. Have a drink?"

"I still got half a workday ahead of me," Slocum said. "I don't need to be getting drunk so early in the day."

"Hell, one drink won't hurt you."

"All right."

Tipton got up and went to his liquor cabinet to pour two glasses of whiskey. Then he carried one of them over to Slocum.

"Thanks," Slocum said.

Tipton raised his glass, and so did Slocum, and they drank.

"Drinking so early in the day?" came a voice.

Slocum looked up to see Jamie smirking at him.

"Just one," he said.

"Well," she said, "bring it on over to the table. Lunch is on."

"Hold on a bit," said Tipton. "Arnie'll be coming along any time now."

Almost as if in answer to his statement, the sounds of

a horse approaching outside came to their ears, and Tipton went to the door and opened it. "You're just in time, Arnie," he called out. "Lunch is on the table. Come on in."

"It ain't often I get invited to eat at the big ranch," said Arnie. Slocum stood up as Arnie walked in the door. Arnie looked at him with curiosity. Tipton was already pouring another glass of whiskey. He walked over to his brother and handed him the glass.

"Arnie," he said, "I want you to meet Slocum. He's working for me. Slocum, this is my brother, Arnold Tipton."

Slocum shook hands with Arnie. "Glad to meet you," he said.

"You must be somebody special," Arnie said, "to be eating in the big house with the family. Lige don't even eat in here."

"Special fence-mender today," Slocum said.

"You men want to come to the table?" said Myrtle. "Hello, Arnie. Welcome."

"Howdy, Myrtle," said Arnie. Jamie came out of the kitchen just then, and Arnie added, "Howdy, Jamie."

"Hello, Uncle Arnie. Glad you could make it."

Arnie, Tipton, and Slocum, taking their glasses with them, moved to the table and sat down. Soon their plates were heaped, and the conversation slowed down as they turned to their meals. In a while, Jamie spoke out.

"Did I hear you say you'd been fixing fence today, Slocum?" she asked.

"Yes, ma'am," he said.

"Well, now, that's not exactly what I understood you'd been hired to do."

"Just what has he been hired to do?" asked Arnie.

"I told Lige," said Slocum, "that when Mr. Tipton didn't need me, I wanted to work. That was the job he set me to do."

"Arnie," said Tipton, "last night, in the Hogneck, Brace Beamer come on me from behind. He was fixing to kill me in cold blood. Slocum here saved me. I figured then and there that if the Beamers are going to be coming at me unexpected, I could use a little help. That's what I hired Slocum for."

"I see," said Arnie. He looked at Slocum sideways. "A bodyguard, huh?"

"That's about it," said Tipton.

"You really think that's necessary?"

"Hell, I just told you what happened."

"Ah, Brace is the really crazy one," Arnie said. "If Slocum killed him—"

"He didn't. He beaned him with a bottle. Brace went to jail for the night."

"Beaned him with a bottle?"

"Yeah. From way across the room. It was the best pitch I ever saw."

Arnie gave Slocum another look, but he didn't say anything more. In another few minutes, everyone was finished with the meal. Jamie poured coffee all around, but Slocum declined. "It's about time for me to get back to work," he said.

"Have some coffee first," said Tipton.

"Yeah," said Arnie. "Who's going to challenge the bodyguard?" Then he laughed.

"I think I'll be going," Slocum said.

"Don't be like that," said Jamie. "I've already poured it." She put the cup down in front of Slocum.

"I reckon I can take time for one cup," Slocum said. "Do you mind if I carry it out on the porch?"

"I'll join you," said Jamie.

"We all will," said Tipton.

"Carl," said Arnie, "I need to talk to you."

"Oh, all right. The rest of you go on out. We'll be along directly."

Slocum and Jamie went out on to the porch and found chairs to sit on.

"I apologize for my uncle," Jamie said. "He was a little rough on you."

"I ain't hurt," Slocum said.

"I know, but what he said wasn't called for."

"He don't like me," said Slocum. "He ain't alone in that."

"Well, I hope you won't let it bother you. He doesn't come around all that often anyway."

"Well," said Slocum, "it don't bother me."

"I think it does," said Jamie. "I heard you offer to go eat with the boys, and you didn't want to hang around long enough to drink a cup of coffee."

"I just felt like I might be in the way," he said. "And right now, I feel like I'm taking too long for lunch. I want to work for my pay just like anyone else."

"That's admirable. Most men would take advantage of the position Daddy gave you."

"I ain't—"

"I know. You ain't most men. By the way, when you said that Arnie didn't like you, and that he wasn't alone in that, I hope you didn't mean to include me."

"Oh, no, ma'am, I—"

"I know I've acted a little smart with you. I was just fooling. I'm sorry if I gave you the impression that I didn't like you."

"No harm's done, ma'am," Slocum said.

Just then Slocum overheard Arnie's voice raised inside the house. "It ain't like I'm over here every week," he said. "Hell, Carl, I just need a little to tide me over. That's all. You can afford it. You with this damn big ranch and all. Things are going to turn around for me here before long, and I'll pay you back. This and everything else I've borrowed."

Slocum picked up his cup to finish the coffee. He stood up and handed the empty cup to Jamie. "I'd best be getting on," he said.

Jamie took the cup. "All right, Slocum," she said. As Slocum went down the stairs, Jamie glanced toward the house with a worried look on her face. Slocum mounted the Appaloosa, tipped his hat, turned and rode off. As he rode, he pondered the situation he had gotten himself into. It was an uncomfortable spot to be in. Jamie had been sarcastic with him at first, but when Arnie had tied into him, she had apologized to him. That had surprised him. He would have expected her to join in with her uncle. The only thing he could make of that was that she had just been teasing. Teasing usually meant just one thing, and Slocum wasn't sure that he didn't like that. She was a fine-looking young woman. He'd have to be careful though. He sure didn't want to get shot by the man he was supposed to be protecting.

Carl liked him all right, and so did Myrtle, and it was Carl, after all, who had hired him. Myrtle was likely happy to have someone guarding her husband from that family of Beamers. But Lige didn't like it, and now it was obvious that Carl's brother Arnie did not like it, either. Well, Jamie had said that Arnie wouldn't be around that much. Maybe it would be all right. But then, Slocum was a bit uncomfortable, too, at having overheard what Arnie was saying to Carl. He felt like he had been eavesdropping on private family concerns. Arnie was obviously useless. He had a ranch but couldn't manage his own affairs. He was bumming money from his brother, and apparently it wasn't the first time. Not only that, he was being rude and insistent about it. Well, that was none of Slocum's business. He did wonder, though, if he had made the right decision in accepting Carl Tipton's offer of a job.

He rode on back to the spot he had abandoned when Lige had come after him for lunch, and he set to work again right away. Working alone like that, he had plenty of time for his thoughts, but he was just thinking the same thing over and over again. He tried to think of something else. He tried to think about Jamie naked. What would she look like? He thought that he had a pretty good imagination when it came to women's bodies, but thinking about Jamie like that made him feel guilty. Carl and Myrtle were both nice folks, and they sure wouldn't like it if they knew he was contemplating their daughter in that manner. He had to think about something else. Anything.

He forced himself to think about his job and the Beamers. How many of them had Tipton said there were? Ten? Ten Beamers to watch out for. And he didn't even know what they looked like except for Brace. Were there any Beamer women, he wondered. What would they be like? It was likely he'd have to kill all of the Beamer men, if they were anything like what Carl Tipton said they were like, and if the rest of them were anything like Brace. Then if they did have any women, what would become of them? Slocum thought that he should find himself another line of work, but it was too late for that just now. Perhaps if he ever finished this job, he would look for something else. Maybe if he rode into some ranch in some part of the country where he had never been before, not wearing his Colt, just pretending to be an ordinary cowhand, maybe he could get a job like that. Then he could just mind his own business and work at his job and stay out of trouble. Maybe. Hell, he knew better than that. He had tried it before.

He worked steadily, and by the end of the day, he had finished his job. He mounted up and headed back for the ranch house. When he arrived and had put up his horse, he found Lige sitting on the porch with Carl Tipton. Each man had a drink in his hand.

"Howdy, Slocum," said Carl. "I'll get you a drink. Pull up a chair."

"Thanks," said Slocum. He dragged a chair over and sat down as Tipton went into the house.

"How's the fence coming?" Lige asked.

"All done," said Slocum.

"All done? There was a heap of fence to take care of out yonder."

"Well, I done it."

"I'll check on it in the morning," said Lige.

"I wish you would," said Slocum.

Just then, Tipton came back out and handed Slocum a drink. Then he resumed his seat.

"Thanks," Slocum said.

"Well, I'll ride out and check on it," said Lige. "If it is all done, I'll find you something else for tomorrow."

"Forget about it," said Tipton. "I need Slocum tomorrow."

Lige looked over at his boss. "You riding out somewhere tomorrow?" he asked.

"I got to go into town, and then I got to ride over to Arnie's place."

"Okay," said Lige. "I guess you'll need your body-guard then for sure."

Slocum took note of the sarcastic tone of Lige's voice. "You'll find that fence is all right," he said.

"Yeah? Well, I'll see. I'll check it over."

Slocum shrugged and tasted his whiskey. It was mighty good. Lige turned his down and put the glass on the porch rail. He stood up.

"I'd better be getting back to the boys," he said.

"All right, Lige," said Tipton. "Have someone saddle up my horse first thing in the morning. Slocum's, too."

"I'll take care of my own horse," said Slocum.

"I'll have yours ready to go, Boss," said Lige, giving Slocum a look. He went down off the porch and started walking toward the bunkhouse.

"He seems like a good man," said Slocum.

"He's the best," said Tipton.

"He sure don't like me worth a damn," said Slocum, "but I tried to put myself in his place. I'd likely feel the same way."

"Don't let it bother you," said Tipton. "Lige will do what I tell him to do."

"I ain't bothered much by it," Slocum said.

"Slocum," said Tipton, "first thing in the morning, we need to head into town. I got some business to take care of at the bank. From there we'll ride out to my brother's place. Then we'll come back here, but it's going to take most of the day to do all that. I just want you to ride along with me is all. Just make sure that no one slips up behind my back."

"Sure thing," said Slocum. "That's what you hired me for."

"I'm not expecting any trouble," said Tipton, "but you never know. Besides the Beamers, when I leave the bank, I'll be carrying some money with me."

"All right."

"I just want you to know what's going on. That's all."

"All right," said Slocum. "I'll be up and ready to go."

The door opened and Jamie stepped out.

"Are you two about ready to eat?" she said. "We've got a mess of vittles ready for you."

"I'm hungry as a bear," said Slocum.

"Well, let's go inside then," said Tipton.

As Slocum stood up and turned to go inside, he noticed that Jamie gave him a smile that looked to him to be a bit more than just friendly.

4

Slocum was up early the next morning and out to saddle his Appaloosa. He found a cowhand saddling another horse. He figured Lige had sent the man to saddle a horse for Carl Tipton. He greeted the man and went on about his business. Then he rode the Appaloosa back to the ranch house and tied it at the hitch rail there. The cowhand he had seen at the corral was just behind him, bringing the other horse. Slocum walked on into the house. He found Tipton coming out of his bedroom.

"Morning, Slocum," Tipton said.

"Good morning, Carl," said Slocum. "Our horses are waiting outside, ready to go."

"Good. We'll just have a quick breakfast here and then we'll be on our way."

Myrtle and Jamie spread out the meal, and they all ate. The conversation at the table was casual. When they finished, they all had one last cup of coffee. Tipton got up brusquely, ready to head out. Slocum followed his lead. They said their good-byes, put on their hats, and headed out the door. Slocum was wearing his Colt. His Winchester was in the saddle boot. Both men mounted up and headed for the main ranch gate. They made their way to the main road which led into town without saying anything. Then Tipton spoke up.

"I feel a little bit foolish, riding into town with a bodyguard, Slocum, but then, you never know what you might run into."

"I wouldn't let it worry me none if I was you," said Slocum.

"Well, I'll admit to you, I do feel somewhat better with you riding along. Those damn Beamers have got me jumpy."

"I'll watch for any sign of trouble the best I can."

"I trust you to do that," said Tipton.

The ride into town took them a couple of hours, and they made it without incident. They hauled up in front of the Breakneck Bank and dismounted. Lapping their reins around the hitch rail there, they walked inside. Tipton walked up to the counter and spoke to a teller there. Slocum hung back and tried not to pay any attention to what was going on. It was none of his business. He was just along as a hired gun. He was pretty sure though that Tipton was getting some money to take to his worthless brother. In just a few minutes, Tipton turned and headed for the front door. Slocum followed him out. Outside, they mounted up again and headed out of town. On the way, Tipton said hello to a few people they passed.

"Arnie has a hard time making ends meet," Tipton suddenly volunteered once they were out on the open road again. "I have to help him out now and then."

"It's none of my business," said Slocum. "I reckon a man has got to help out his family some."

"Arnie's younger than me," said Tipton. "I was out here first. A few years after I got good and established, Arnie come out. He decided that he wanted to do the same thing that I had done, but he just can't seem to get ahead. I know it frustrates him, watching how well I'm doing. I invited him to sell out and come in with me, but he won't do it. He thinks he has to make it on his own."

"Some men have to learn the hard way," Slocum said, and as soon as he had said it, he thought better of it. But Tipton didn't seem to pay any attention to it. They were riding out of Breakneck in a different direction from which they had gone in, and it took them another two hours or so to reach Arnie Tipton's ranch. Slocum immediately noticed the run-down condition of the place. Fences needed mending. There was junk in the yard. The house could have used some good, hard work. Arnie heard them coming, for he was out the front door before they had stopped. As they reined in, he spoke up first.

"You brought Slocum along, I see," he said.

"Howdy, Mr. Tipton," said Slocum.

Arnie ignored him and spoke to his brother. "Our business is private," he said. "Come inside."

"I won't be long, Slocum," said Carl Tipton, dismounting and following his brother to the front door.

"Take your time," Slocum said. "I'm all right."

"Hell, yeah, he's on the payroll, ain't he?" said Arnie, going through the door. The older Tipton followed him inside. Still sitting in his saddle, Slocum took out a cigar and lit it. He tried not to think about the relationship between the two brothers. It was none of his business. But he couldn't stop himself. Arnie was a worthless bastard, he thought. That was all there was to it. He wondered why a fairly decent man like Carl Tipton had to be saddled with a worthless shit like that for a younger brother. He looked around. The spread was not bad. He could see no reason why a man couldn't make a go of it. Arnie had to be lazy and shiftless or just plain stupid. Maybe all of that. He had good grass, and apparently he had water. Slocum puffed on his cigar and tried to make his mind think of something else, but when he tried that, all he could come up with was Jamie. He wondered if he should move on down the road. Maybe he would. Tonight, he said to himself, he would tell Tipton that he had decided to move along. He wouldn't even take any of the old man's money. He'd just ride out first thing in the morning. Arnie and Jamie spoiled the whole deal.

By and by, Carl Tipton came out the door. He walked to his horse and mounted up. Before they could turn their horses to ride out, Arnie stepped out the door. "See you later, brother," he said. "Slocum, don't strain yourself now."

Slocum fought an urge to say something to the younger Tipton. What he really wanted to do was to get down off his horse and smack the silly little shit across the face. Just slap him like the unruly punk he was. But instead he just kept quiet and rode along with Carl Tipton. Carl said, "Take care, Arnie."

They moved back out onto the road, and Slocum was biting his tongue. He really had some things to say about the snotty Arnie, but he knew that he had better just keep quiet. It wouldn't do to cuss the boss's brother.

"I wish that boy'd grow up," Carl muttered.

Slocum thought that Arnie looked to be at least forty-five, but he still kept quiet. The ride into town, out to Arnie's and back to the ranch looked like it was going to take up the best part of the day. Slocum wanted to tell old Carl to leave the damn sponger alone. Then maybe he'd have to grow up. Stop giving him money. If he can't make a go of the ranch, then let him sell the damn thing and find something else to do. But he knew that it would do no good. He would just stick to his plan to leave first thing in the morning. Before breakfast even.

They rounded a curve in the road and found themselves looking at two riders who were just sitting there blocking the way. They stopped. Slocum tensed for action.

"Let us pass, boys," said Tipton. "We ain't looking for no trouble."

"You are trouble, Tipton," said one of the riders.

"Slocum," said Tipton, "these here are Beamers."

"I can't say I'm pleased to meet you," said Slocum.

"The lack of pleasure is mutual," said one of the Beamers. "Why don't you just ride on. We got no quarrel with you. Don't even know you."

"You got a brother named Brace?" Slocum asked.

"He's my brother," said one. "I'm Billy. This here's our cousin, Ike."

"Well, I'm going to give you a quarrel with me. Is Brace still in jail?"

"He is."

"Well, I'm the one that put him there. It was me that beaned him with a bottle."

"You?" said Billy.

"You son of a bitch," said Ike.

"That's me," said Slocum. "Mr. Tipton, you just sit tight." He urged his horse out ahead of Tipton, watching the two Beamers carefully as he rode. "Now you two can turn around and ride out of here and stay alive a little longer if you've a mind to. Otherwise, you can go right on ahead and die right here."

"That's mighty big talk, mister," said Ike.

"It's up to you," Slocum said.

"It's two against two," said Tipton.

"No, sir," said Slocum. "You stay back. It's two to one. Just the way I like it."

He noticed Billy lick his lips. Both Beamers looked worried. His bold talk was making them nervous, and that had been his plan.

"I'm tired of waiting around for you to make up your minds," he said, moving a little closer.

"Billy?" said Ike.

"Take him," said Billy, going for his sidearm.

In a flash, Slocum's Colt was out and spitting fire. His first bullet smashed into Billy's chest. His second hit Ike in the left jaw, tearing through his head. Ike hit the ground first. He was still alive and moaning, writhing on the ground. Billy was still in the saddle with a hole in his chest, blood spurting out of the hole. His head lolled. His chin dropped onto his chest. His whole body relaxed then, and he slowly slid from the saddle and fell like a sack of manure onto the road. Slocum knew that Billy was done for. He looked at Ike. He could load him up and take him to a doctor, but he knew that Ike wouldn't last the journey. He'd bleed to death along the way and be miserable the whole time. He raised his Colt and fired a third shot, hitting Ike in the chest and killing him instantly. He looked back at Tipton.

"You want to load them up and take them to town?" he asked.

"Yeah," said Tipton. "I reckon we ought to."

Through the big, front window of his office, Seth Willis saw the two riders stop out in the street. He also saw the two horses they were leading with the loads they were carrying: two bodies. He did not wait for them to dismount and come into the office. He shoved back his chair

and stood up, grabbing his hat as he walked out the door.
When he appeared on the sidewalk, Tipton said, "Howdy,
Seth."

"Carl," said Willis, "what's this all about?"

"You can see who they are," said Tipton.

Willis stepped down into the street and walked around
to get a better look.

"Beamers," he said. "Ike and Billy."

"That's right."

"Tell me how it happened."

"They were waiting in the trail for Mr. Tipton," said
Slocum. "They stated their intentions pretty clear."

"They meant to kill him?" said Willis.

"Damn right they did," said Tipton. "Told Slocum to
just ride on and leave me to them."

"Well, it's obvious that he didn't do that," said Willis.

"I killed them," said Slocum.

"Both of them?"

"That's right."

"Who drew first?"

"Billy."

"You were facing them?"

"Sitting on horseback."

"That's damn fast shooting, Slocum," Willis said. "Not
that I doubt your word. Especially when it's backed by
Carl Tipton. But it's damn fast."

"That's why I'm still alive," Slocum said.

"You need anything more from us?" asked Tipton.

"No. I guess not," Willis said. "You can go on."

"We didn't have to bring them in," said Slocum.

"I know," said Willis. "I appreciate it."

"Slocum," said Tipton, "how about a drink in the Hogneck?"

"Suits me."

They rode their horses down the street to the saloon
and tied them there at the rail. Then they went inside.
Several people greeted Tipton, and he introduced Slocum
to a few of them. Then he paid for a bottle and took it
and two glasses to a table. They sat down. Tipton poured
the drinks and shoved one over toward Slocum. Slocum

took it and downed it at once. Tipton refilled it.

"Killing do that to you?" he asked.

"Talking to sheriffs," said Slocum.

Tipton laughed. He took a drink of his own whiskey. Slocum took a sip of his second. "It's good. Thanks," he said.

"You're welcome," said Tipton. "And Slocum, thank you. You saved my life out there again today. And Willis was right. You were incredibly fast with that Colt. How'd you get that way?"

"Just lots of practice," Slocum said. "Combined with a powerful will to live. That's all."

"No secret to it?"

"No secret."

"Slocum, there's no need in my telling you how glad I am that you were along with me today. I'm no gun-fighter. Those two would've left my body laying in the road out there. That's a fact."

Slocum took another drink. He knew that Tipton was right about that. And there were still other Beamers to worry about. Hell, he thought, I guess I can put up with what I have to from Lige and Arnie. And Jamie. Even that. He told himself that he could not keep his promise to himself about riding out in the morning. Twice now he had seen Beamers attempt to murder old Tipton. And there were still more of them. There would be more at-tempts. He was sure of that. No. He would stick around and see it through. Seth Willis came walking in just then. He moved straight to the table where Tipton and Slocum were sitting.

"Pull up a chair, Seth," said Tipton. The sheriff pulled out a chair and sat down.

"Well, Carl," he said, "it looks like you made the right move in hiring Slocum on."

"I sure as hell did."

"Slocum, I didn't mean to be short with you a while ago. I'm glad that you were with Carl. The Beamers are no good, and Carl's a friend of mine. I sure wouldn't want to see them get him."

"I just did my job," Slocum said.

"He did it damn good, too," said Tipton.

"I've seen Billy in action," said Willis. "He was pretty good."

"Not good enough," Tipton said.

"Well, maybe this will make the rest of the tribe think twice before they try to pull anything else on you."

"That's what worries me," Slocum said.

"What do you mean by that?"

"They've tried twice now. Next time, they might decide to be more sneaky about it."

"Like shoot from hiding?" said Willis.

"Something like that."

"Yeah. Well, you might be interested to know that they'll all likely be in town tomorrow."

"What for?" Tipton asked.

"Brace will be tried tomorrow for attempting to kill you the other night. He could be sent to prison. His whole family'll be in to see what happens."

"You expecting trouble from them?" said Tipton.

"That's the sensible way to look at it," said Willis.

5

Slocum again rode into Breakneck with Tipton the following day to attend the trial. Lige had offered to ride
along, but Tipton had told him to stay behind and take
care of the ranch. "Slocum's all I need," the old man had
said. That seemed to irritate Lige, Slocum noted, but nothing more was said. In town, they found the saloon, which
was doubling as a courthouse, packed. They made their
way in and found seats near the front of the room. Slocum
noticed a whole crowd of rough-looking rannies glaring
at him and Tipton. Sitting right in the middle of the gang
was an old woman. She glared the hardest. Slocum leaned
over to speak low in Tipton's ear.

"Would that be the rest of the Beamers over yonder?"
he asked.

Tipton glanced and answered, "That's them, all right.
And a couple of extras thrown in for boot."

"Oh?"

"Yeah. Them two on the far right. I never seen them
before. Might be some relatives come out to join them.
Might be some hands they hired on to help with the rus-
tling and killing. They're with the Beamers though. That
much is clear."

"Yeah," Slocum said. So counting Brace, there were
eight Beamers, and counting the two strangers with them,
there were still ten to worry about. He didn't worry about
the old woman. The crowd was noisy, almost boisterous,
even though the bar was closed. There was no liquor in

34

sight except the bottles on the shelves against the wall behind the bar. And there was a guard at each end of the bar to keep anyone from going back there. There were a couple of guards at the front door, too. They had taken Slocum's Colt when he came in. They were taking everyone's guns away. Seth Willis and the judge were taking no chances with this trial. Slocum looked the crowd over carefully. In addition to the one at the front door and the two at the bar, he found four more armed deputies, one in each corner of the room.

At last the judge came in. The crowd was quieted down, and things got started. The charges were read and opening arguments were made. The jury was already seated, having been selected previously. The prosecutor was Mr. Abel Fearing, and the defense attorney was Mr. John Ghost. Fearing was somewhat pompous, rearing back and hooking his thumbs in the armholes of his vest. Ghost was a slimey-looking character, a fitting lawyer for the likes of the Beamers. At last, Slocum was called to the stand by the prosecutor. After some preliminary questions, Fearing asked, "Now, Mr. Slocum, will you tell the court just why in hell you tossed that bottle and beaned Brace Beamer on the noggin?"

"Well, sir," Slocum said, "I could see that the man had a gun out and was fixing to do a murder on Mr. Tipton."

"Objection," called out Ghost. "How could Mr. Slocum tell what my client's intention was?"

"The man said, 'I'm going to kill you, Tipton,' " Slocum said.

The crowd roared with laughter, and the judge rapped his gavel on the table vigorously. At last the laughter subsided, and the judge said, "Proceed."

"So you saw that Mr. Tipton was about to be shot, and you threw the bottle?" said Fearing.

"That's right."

"I have no further questions of this witness," Fearing said.

"Mr. Ghost?" said the judge.

Ghost stood up and slithered over to the chair where Slocum was seated. He hawked a great gob of nastiness up from his lungs and spat in the spittoon near the bar. He harrumphed. "Slocum," he said, "how did you come to know Mr. Brace Beamer?"

"I don't know him," Slocum said.

"You don't know him?"

"Never met him. I'd never seen him before the night we're talking about here."

"Never met the man. Had never seen the man. Yet you threw a bottle more than half full of good whiskey and knocked him in the head. Did it ever occur to you that you might have killed him like that?"

"I suppose I could have," said Slocum, "but I figured he'd have a better chance than if I shot him."

"Indeed. So you chose to intervene yourself in this fight between Mr. Beamer and Carl Tipton on account of your acquaintance with the latter?"

"If you mean Mr. Tipton," Slocum said, "I'd never seen him before that, either."

"What's that? You were unacquainted with either of the parties involved in the fracas?"

"I didn't know either one of them," Slocum said, "and I didn't see no fracas, either."

"Well, just what did you see that caused you to interfere in a private argument?"

"I didn't hear no argument. I seen a man with a cocked gun in his hand fixing to shoot an unarmed man, and I thought to prevent a cold-blooded murder. And I think that I done that."

Seth Willis was called, and he said that he did not see anything. When he came into the saloon, Brace Beamer was lying flat on his back, out cold. He had interviewed Slocum and Tipton and gotten the same story that Slocum had told in court. Other witnesses to the event corroborated Slocum's story. Tipton was called to the stand.

"Brace Beamer came up behind me," he said. "He pulled his six-gun and cocked it. Then he called me by name. I turned around to find him pointing his shooter at me. He said that he intended to kill me then and there, and that's when Mr. Slocum went into action."

"What do you mean by 'went into action'?" asked Fearing.

"He tossed the bottle."

Ghost got up to cross-examine. "Mr. Tipton," he said, "were you acquainted with Mr. Slocum before that night?"

"No, sir."

"How come, do you think, he chose to interfere on your behalf?"

"I take his word that he just wanted to prevent a murder."

"Well, it's a rare thing to find a Good Samaratin these days, ain't it? Mr. Tipton, is it true that you've hired on Slocum as a personal bodyguard?"

"It is. I figured—"

"And is it true that your personal bodyguard just yesterday on the public road went and killed Ike and Billy Beamer?"

"Yes. They was—"

"No more questions, Mr. Tipton. It seems as how Slocum has got a vendetta against the Beamer family. That's all."

"Objection!" shouted Fearing. The crowd roared. The judge beat the table hard with his gavel. At last the crowd was quieted again. There were no more witnesses to be called. It was time for the lawyers to make their summations. Fearing went first. He stood up and paraded back and forth in front of the jury in silence. At last he spoke.

"Members of the jury," he said, "this case is clear. Brace Beamer attempted to do a murder on Mr. Carl Tipton. There were witnesses to that fact. Had he not been interfered with, he would have shot Mr. Tipton to death right then and there. The charge in this case is attempted murder, and you have no choice but to render a verdict of guilty. Now, Mr. Ghost is going to try his best to confuse you with matters that have nothing to do with this case. Ignore his clumsy attempts. You have nothing to consider except the events that took place in the Hogneck Saloon on the night in question. Brace Beamer took out his weapon and cocked it. He aimed it at Mr. Tipton, who was unarmed, and declared his intentions of killing Mr. Tipton then and there, and would have done so had not Mr. Slocum stopped him. Guilty, gentlemen, guilty."

"Mr. Ghost," said the judge.

Ghost stood up and looked at his papers for a moment. Then he tossed them down on the table and walked over to the jury. He hemmed and hawed, and he spat into the spittoon.

"Gentlemen of the jury," he said, "this here is obvious a case of the rich and privileged ganging up on the poor and deprived. Just the other day, I heard, Tipton had some of his cowhands gang up on one of the Beamers and rope him and drag him behind a running horse. Then when there was a little argument in the saloon between Brace Beamer and Carl Tipton, Tipton's personal bodyguard bashed in Beamer's head with a full bottle of whiskey and like to have killed him. The sheriff, siding with the rich, put poor Brace in jail and charged him with attempted murder. Hell, members of the jury, it looks like to me that Brace is the one that like to have got killed. Then just yesterday, this same Slocum went and killed two of the Beamers, poor ole Ike and Billy. We all knew Ike and Billy. Good boys they was."

"Mr. Ghost," said the judge, "I'm inclined to give you leeway in your summation, but you are going too far by bringing in matters that do not pertain to this trial."

"I'm all done, your honor, sir," Ghost said. "Except to just tell the jury that what I think ought to happen here is I think that the judge had ought to just dismiss the charges in this case and throw it out of court. But since he don't show no inclination to do that, then I say that you should take things into your own hands and do what's right by bringing in a verdict of not guilty. That's all."

The judge then admonished the jury to disregard all of Ghost's comments about Ike and Billy, and then he charged the bailiff with taking the jury out to deliberate. They were gone for an hour. While they waited, Slocum and Tipton went outside to smoke cigars.

"Where'd they find that damned Ghost fellow?" Slocum asked.

"He's got his office right here in Breakneck," said Tipton. "They've used him before. Every crook and bum around uses him. He's a no-good sleazy son of a bitch."

"That's pretty clear," said Slocum. "What about the jury?"

"I know them all," Tipton said. "They're all pretty good ole boys."

When they saw the jury returning, Tipton and Slocum went back inside and resumed their seats. The jury got settled back in, and the judge called for the verdict. The foreman stood up.

"How do you find?" asked the judge.

"Well, your honor," said the foreman, "we find the defendant, Brace Beamer, sort of guilty."

"Sort of? What do you mean by that?"

"Well, he was the only one that really got hurt."

"That is not a legal verdict," the judge said. "Bailiff, take them out again, and this time when you come back, I want to hear a verdict of guilty or of not guilty. Do you understand that?"

"Yes, your honor," said the foreman of the jury, "but I don't reckon we have to go out again."

He leaned over and whispered to other members of the jury. They all nodded their heads in agreement. Some of them shrugged. The foreman straightened up again.

"We find him guilty, your honor," he said.

"This court is recessed until ten o'clock tomorrow morning. We'll have sentencing then." The judge rapped his gavel, and someone stood up and shouted, "The bar's open." There was a general rush for the bar. The sheriff took Brace Beamer and walked him through the crowd to go back to the jail. Slocum and Tipton went back to the door where Slocum retrieved his Colt, and they went outside to mount up and ride back out to the ranch. Tipton was in the saddle. Slocum was about to swing up when he heard his name called. He looked around to see the Beamers, all but Brace, gathered up on the sidewalk.

"Your days are numbered, Slocum, you dirty son of a bitch," said one of them.

Slocum looked at the man. He swung up into the saddle. "Could be yours are, too," he said. "All of you."

"You threatening to kill us all, Slocum?"

"One at a time or all of you at once," Slocum said. "It don't matter to me. Right now or later. It's your choice."

"Leave off, Hump," said the old woman. "This ain't the time nor place for it."

"Hell," said the one called Hump. "There's too many witnesses here. They'd say we ganged up on you. But we'll meet again, Slocum. You can be sure of that."

"Hell," said Slocum, "I'll be looking forward to it."

The Beamers turned and ambled back into the saloon, a couple of them looking back over their shoulders to scowl at Slocum. Tipton pulled his watch out of his vest pocket and looked at it.

"Slocum," he said, "there's a pretty good place to eat down the street. What do you say?"

Slocum shrugged. "I'm agreeable," he said.

He followed Tipton down the street to a place called Harmony's Eats. They dismounted and hitched their horses to the rail in front. Then they went inside. It was a small place but clean. There were a few customers inside eating, but not many. Most folks were still over in the Hogneck Saloon. Tipton found them a table and he and Slocum sat down. In just a couple of minutes a good-looking waitress with shoulder-length brown hair appeared at their table. Slocum figured her to be in her thirties. She smiled down at them, and Slocum liked the looks of the smile, the whole package.

"Hello, Carl," she said. "Who's the stranger?"

"Harmony," said Tipton, "this here is Slocum. He's working for me."

"Howdy, Slocum," Harmony said. "Welcome. Well, what can I do for you boys?"

"Bring us some coffee," Tipton said, "and whatever good you got to eat today."

"I've got some damn good beef stew."

"That'll do," said Tipton.

"Sounds good to me," said Slocum.

"Be right out."

Slocum watched the swing of Harmony's hips as she

walked away. Now there was something to take his mind off his troubles. If he could get better acquainted with Harmony, that might keep him from thinking so much about Jamie. He was getting tired of trying to hold himself at bay on that matter, not wanting to get into trouble with his boss. Yes, this Harmony looked like a fine thing to Slocum.

"Slocum," said Tipton, "I believe I can read your mind."

"Yeah," said Slocum, "I expect you can. Is she married or spoke for?" He was thinking, though, that he hoped the old man had not been reading his mind before this.

"Neither one," said Tipton. "She's free for the taking."

Slocum started to ask another question, but he saw Harmony coming back with a tray. She put down two cups of coffee, two spoons, and two big bowls of beef stew. She placed a chunk of bread in the middle of the table. "There you go," she said. "If you need anything else, give a holler."

"Anything?" said Slocum, a bit suggestively.

"Ahh," she said, looking back at him and wagging a finger, but she was still smiling. That was a good sign. He liked a woman who could take some teasing, but then, there was always the danger that she wouldn't want to let it go any farther than teasing. He hoped that he would have a chance to find out if Harmony was that type or not. Somehow he did not think that she would be. Only time would tell.

"Nothing like being obvious," Tipton said.

Slocum shrugged and picked up his spoon. He took a big bite of the stew. It was hot.

"It's good," he said. "It's hot, too."

His eyes were watering. Tipton laughed and spooned some out for himself. Instead of shoving it in his mouth, he blew on it. Slocum pulled a bit of bread off the chunk in the middle of the table.

"So," he said, "how come a good-looking woman like that is in this town and not already branded?"

"I don't rightly know," said Tipton. "She come to town a year or so ago with a little money and bought this place.

No one knows where she come from or anything else about her for that matter. A few boys has tried, but she's just run them off. It's like she ain't got no use for men."

"Maybe she just never run across the right one," said Slocum.

"You think you might be that right one?"

"There's nothing like trying," Slocum said.

6

It was later that same night, well after Slocum and Tipton had returned to the ranch and well after the Hogneck had closed its doors. Breakneck looked almost like a ghost town. The sidewalks had been rolled up tight. There wasn't a human being in sight, not even a horse tied on the street. Nine Beamers rode slowly into town, or at least, seven Beamers and their two unknown recent recruits. They rode slowly up to the jail and dismounted, tying their horses—along with an extra one, saddled—loosely to the hitch rail in front. They looked at one another with grim and determined expressions on their unshaven faces, peering out from under the floppy, wide brims of their hats. Then the one in the lead stepped up onto the sidewalk. The others followed. The leader pulled out his six-gun, and the others did the same. He glanced around one last time, and he said, "You ready?"

"We're ready, Hump," one of them answered.

Hump tried the door but found it locked. He lifted his six-gun and pounded the door with its butt. The noise resounded in the seemingly abandoned town. When there was no immediate response, he pounded again. At last there came an answer from inside.

"Who is it?"

"Charlie Hope," Hump Beamer answered. "I ride for Mister Tipton. We got troubles out here."

"Just a minute."

Inside the jail, Seth Willis pulled on his trousers and

43

lifted the suspenders up onto his shoulders. He headed for the door. He hesitated and went back for his revolver. Then he went to open the door. He shoved back the latch and pulled on the handle. "Charlie," he said, "what—"

He stopped, for he was looking, not at Charlie Hope, but instead at the ugly mug of Hump Beamer and at the muzzle of Hump's six-gun. Before he had time to react, Hump pulled the trigger, and a piece of lead tore into Willis's chest. Willis staggered back, an expression of disbelief on his face. Then he sagged onto the floor to lie in a pool of spreading blood. Hump strode into the office, stepping over the body of Seth Willis and stomping on across to the desk. The rest of his gang followed him.

"Hump," called Brace from the cell, "get me the hell out of here."

"Hold your horses, Brace," Hump said. "I'm just getting the keys."

He rummaged around on the desk till he found the key ring. Grabbing it up, he headed for the cell. Two of the other Beamers stood by the front door looking out onto the street.

"Hurry it up," one of them said.

"You see anyone coming?" Hump asked.

"No, but someone's bound to have heard that shot."

"Just keep your britches on," Hump said.

Hump tried one key and it didn't work. He tried another.

"Hurry up, Hump."

"Shut the fuck up. I'm moving as fast as I can."

He tried a third key, and the lock clicked and turned. He jerked open the door. Brace came rushing out. Another Beamer was going through desk drawers. He found Brace's gunbelt with the six-gun still in the holster, and he handed it to Brace. Brace wrapped the belt around his waist and started to fasten the buckle.

"Come on," said the man at the door.

Brace finished fastening the buckle and headed for the door. Already most of the gang was outside mounting up. The mounted men all looked nervously up and down the street. Brace went out and climbed onto the extra horse.

The last one out was Hump. He stopped in the doorway and looked back at Seth Willis lying still on the floor. For good measure, he fired one more round into the helpless sheriff. Then he rushed on out to his waiting horse and climbed up into the saddle.

"Let's get the hell out of here," he shouted. They all turned their mounts and headed out of Breakneck at a fast pace. "Yahoo!" yelled Brace.

Back in the jail, Seth Willis moaned and tried to move. He could not. He had dropped his gun with Hump Beamer's first shot and it was lying on the floor within a foot of his right hand. He opened his eyes and saw the revolver. He stretched out his hand. It was beyond his reach. He tried to crawl toward it, but he could not move. He sucked in a few deep breaths, each one hurting like hell, and then he mustered all his remaining strength to reach for the gun. His fingers managed to touch the handle, and he worked the revolver toward him. At last he was able to grasp the handle. He got his finger on the trigger and his thumb on the hammer. It took a mighty effort, but he pulled back the hammer and fired a shot. Then he cocked the piece again and fired again. The effort had been almost too much for him. He relaxed and blacked out.

Outside, two men appeared on the street. One was in a nightshirt carrying a shotgun. The other was just tucking his shirttail into his britches. They looked at one another.

"You hear them shots?" said one.

"Sounded like they come from the sheriff's office."

"Let's get over there and see."

The two men rushed across the street and found the front door to the sheriff's office open. They looked at one another, and then one of the two poked his face inside the open door.

"My God," he said. "Someone's shot Seth."

"Is he dead?"

"I ain't sure. Run and get the doc."

The other man turned and ran. There were a few more men on the street by then, and as he ran, he called out, "Someone's shot Seth. I'm going for Doc."

The other men ran on inside the jail.

"Say," said one, "they broke ole Brace out of jail."

"It must've been the Beamers that done it then."

"Let's get Seth up off the floor," said one. "We can lay him on the cot in the cell."

Doc stepped in just then and saw what was happening. "Be careful with him," he said. "That's it. Get him on that cot. Someone light a lamp. Hurry it up. I got to be able to see what I'm doing."

They got Willis onto the cot and Doc shoved them aside getting to his patient. First he put his head on the sheriff's chest listening. When he straightened up, there was blood on the side of his face.

"How is he, Doc?"

"Well, he's not dead, but he's not far from it."

He tore open the sheriff's shirt and reached for his bag.

Outside of town, the Beamers rode hard for their own ranch headquarters. They ran their horses up to the corral, unsaddled them, and turned them loose. Then they started walking toward the house. The scraggly, tough-looking old woman stepped out the front door as they approached.

"Brace," she said. "Come here, boy."

Brace rushed up to the old woman, and she embraced him, squeezing him tightly. Brace put his own arms around her.

"I'm all right, Maw," he said.

"Oh, I'm so glad to see you. I couldn't bear the thought of seeing you in prison. I'd as soon have saw you dead."

"Well, I ain't dead, Maw, and I ain't in prison, neither. Thanks to Hump and the boys."

The old woman at last released Brace. She looked around at the rest of the brood. "Hump," she said, "you done good. All of you done good. I'm proud of you. Did you have any trouble?"

"Hell," said one of the boys, "there wasn't anyone in town awake."

They all laughed. "I had to shoot ole Seth," Hump said.

"You kill him?" asked the old woman.

"He looked dead to me. I shot him twice."

"Good. Anyone else see you?"

"Nary a soul."

"Then there ain't no witnesses, and no one can prove you done it. If anyone comes out this way, we'll just hide Brace and say we don't know nothing about it."

"Maw," said Brace, "I can't stay hid out here forever."

"Just for awhile, sonny boy. Till we see how this thing is going to play out. It won't be long. I promise you. Come on in the house. I got some vittles waiting. Coffee's ready."

"Coffee?" said Brace. "How about whiskey?"

"We got that, too. Come on now."

The boys all followed Maw into the house and grabbed chairs, mostly around a table which stood in the middle of the room. The old woman began spooning out food onto plates and serving them around. A couple of the boys poured themselves cups of coffee, but Brace called out again for the whiskey. Hump found the bottle and some glasses and began pouring them full. They all began drinking whiskey and shoveling food into their mouths.

"Now that we got Brace safe home again," the old woman said, "we got some serious business to be took care of."

"What you thinking about, Maw?" Hump said.

"We got to take care of that damned Tipton and his hired gunfighter."

"That Slocum?" said Brace.

"That one," Maw said. "He killed Billy and Ike. Shot them down like dogs in the road. We can't let men like that live. Slocum for killing them boys and Tipton for hiring him to do it."

"Well, hell, Maw," said Hump. "We got the sheriff tonight. We could hit the Tipton ranch right away while they ain't expecting nothing. Get Tipton and Slocum both."

"No. That's too dangerous. They got too many cowhands over there. One of you boys might get hurt. Killed even. I don't want to lose no more of my boys. Not even to get them two bastards. We got to be clever about this."

"Well, what'll we do then?"

"I'm thinking on it," the old woman said.

Everything was silent then for a time except for the slurping and chawing of the Beamer boys. Then the old hag spoke up again.

"I got it," she said. "I want four of you boys to ride over to Tipton's spread. Hide across the road from his main gate and wait there. Wait till you see them ride out on their way to town or to someplace. Not just anyone. Tipton and Slocum."

"They'll likely be riding into town in the morning thinking they'll listen to my sentencing," said Brace.

"Good," said the old woman. "You're right about that. Take along your rifles with you. When they ride out, you cut them down."

"Let me go, Maw," Brace said. "I got more reason than anyone else. Hell, my head still hurts from where that damn Slocum hit me."

Maw leaned over Brace from behind and put her arms around him. "My poor baby," she said. "Of course you can go. And whoever else goes along with him, you be sure and let him shoot that Slocum. You hear me? Let him kill that no-good gunfighter."

"Sure, Maw," said Hump. "I'm going, too. We'll take along Harman and Hiram with us."

"All right then. Couple of you other boys go out and saddle up four fresh horses. It's about time they got going. Get on now and do it."

Two of the Beamer boys got up and, stuffing their mouths first, headed for the door. In a few more minutes, they returned. "The horses is ready, Maw," one of them said. Brace stood up. He wiped his mouth with his sleeve.

"All right, boys," he said, "let's go do some killing."

Brace, Hump, Harman, and Hiram all headed for the door, but not before Maw gave Brace another tight hug and kissed him on the lips. "You boys be real careful," she said. "I don't want none of you getting hurt, and I don't want my baby boy back in no jail, neither. Hear?"

"Don't worry, Maw," said Hump. "I'll watch out for them."

They left the house, mounted up, and moved out into

the road. Then they turned toward the Tipton spread. It was a ride of a couple of hours, and they figured they'd get there just before sunup. That would give them time to hide their horses and find good spots for themselves to snug down in and hide till they saw Tipton and Slocum come riding out on their way to town.

"I can't wait to kill me that Slocum," said Brace. "My damn head still hurts."

"Don't go getting too anxious now," said Hump. "You be sure of your shot before you take it. Getting over-anxious is what put you in jail in the first place."

"Aw, hell, I was just drunked up then is all. They didn't have no business putting me on trial for that. Wasn't no one hurt. No one 'cept just me is all. I got hurt and they put me on trial. Can you believe that?"

Harman sniggered at that.

"What's so damn funny?" snapped Brace. "It's the truth. Hell, ole Ghost even said it in court. He wouldn't say nothing in court 'less it was true, would he, Hump? Would he?"

"No, hell, I reckon not. But you mind what I say. Be damn sure of your shot before you take it."

"I will. You don't have to worry about me none. The only thing is, I don't want him to die right off. I'd like to wing him real good where he can't shoot, and then walk over to him and let him get a good look at me. I want him to know who done it, and I want him to suffer some in the dying."

"You ain't going to have that kind of choice, little brother," said Hump. "Now you do what I say. When you see that Slocum come riding out onto the road, you drop him dead with one shot. If you ain't going to do that, you best turn around right now and get your ass back home. Slocum's a gunfighter and a damned good one. Don't forget, he took Billy and Ike all by hisself, facing them straight on. You got to show respect for that kind of a gunfighter."

"Show respect?" said Brace.

"Yeah. Shoot from ambush and shoot to kill."

Hump dropped back a little on purpose, allowing Brace

to ride ahead. He managed to get himself alongside Harman. He rode along like that for a ways. Then he leaned over toward Harman and spoke low.

"Harman, if Brace shoots Slocum and don't kill him, you shoot to kill. You got that? You shoot Slocum second and shoot fast."

"I got you," said Harman.

They reached the Tipton ranch and turned into the trees and brush across the road. The trees were too thick to ride through with any degree of comfort, so Hump dismounted, and the others followed his lead. Taking his horse by the reins, Hump moved far back away from the road. At last he stopped.

"We'll tie them up here," he said, and they all did. Then Hump led the way back toward the road. He personally selected spots for each of the other three, spots where they could get down and hide and still have a good view and a good shot of the main gate to and from the Tipton ranch. Then he found his own place and settled in. He checked his weapons and then looked back at the gate. It was about an hour before they saw any sign of life. A lone rider came toward the gate from the direction of the ranch house. When he at last arrived at the gate and turned onto the road, Hump recognized the foreman of the Tipton ranch, Lige Phillips. He casually wondered what Phillips was doing heading into town so early and by himself, but he relaxed. It wasn't Phillips he was after. Suddenly a shot rang out and Phillips jerked in the saddle. Then a second shot sounded. Phillips jerked again. Hump stood up quickly and looked toward where Brace and Harman were secreted. Both men were standing up, firing their rifles. Phillips was hit four or five times before he fell from the saddle.

"Goddamn it," shouted Hump. "That ain't who we wanted."

"Hell," said Brace, "he was one of them."

"Let's get the hell out of here," said Hump. "Our secret's out now for sure."

7

"Well, Slocum," said Tipton as he mounted up in front of the house, "we'll find out what kind of justice we get in Breakneck these days."

"They sure ought to give ole Brace some jail time at least," said Slocum. He was already in the saddle, and he waited for Tipton to turn his horse and head for the main gate. The two men headed on toward the road.

"They're bound to give him something," said Tipton. "I'm just worried about whether it'll be enough."

"We'll find out soon," said Slocum.

They rode on in silence, and when they came close to the gate, Tipton reined in his horse and stared ahead.

"What is it?" said Slocum.

"Up there ahead in the road," said Tipton. "It's a riderless horse just standing there."

"Come on," said Slocum, kicking the Appaloosa in the sides.

"Hold it," Tipton shouted. "It might be a trick."

Slocum slowed his horse's gait, but he moved on toward the road and the horse that was just standing there. Tipton moved along behind him.

"Hey," he called out, "that's one of mine."

Slocum slipped the Colt out of its holster and moved ahead cautiously. At the gate he stopped and dismounted, looking around carefully as he did so. Tipton pulled up beside him and looked at the body lying in the road.

"My God, Slocum," he said, "it's Lige."

"Stay where you are, Carl," Slocum said. He walked over to the body and checked it. Then he looked up again. "He's dead, Carl. Shot full of holes."

"Goddamn it."

Slocum looked around on the other side of the road until he was satisfied that no one was yet lurking there. Then he went back to the body. He looked over at Tipton.

"What do you want to do with him?" he asked.

"Let's load him up and take him back to the house," Tipton said. "Then we'll go on into town and tell Seth what happened. Go on to court after that."

Slocum caught the loose horse, and they loaded Lige's body across the saddle. Then they rode back to the ranch house. They laid Lige out on the porch and covered him. Tipton saw Randy Self over by the corral and called out to him. Randy came over to the porch and saw what had happened. Tipton told him to let all the hands know about it. "We'll have the burying this evening," he said. Then he and Slocum mounted up again and headed on for town.

They stopped by the sheriff's office and found the door standing open. Walking inside, they saw the cell door also standing wide open. There was no one around.

"Maybe Seth's already taken Brace over to the Hogneck," Tipton said. "Let's get on over there."

They climbed back into their saddles and turned their mounts toward the saloon. Along the way, they saw the judge walking down the sidewalk away from the Hogneck. Tipton turned his horse and rode close to the sidewalk.

"Aubrey," he said.

The judge stopped walking and looked up toward Tipton.

"Hello, Carl," he said. "Have you heard the news?"

"What news is that?"

"Someone broke into the jailhouse last night and busted Brace Beamer loose. They shot Seth. Looks like we won't have a sentencing today."

"The Beamers," said Tipton.

"Well, now, we don't know that for sure," said Aubrey. "It sure does look bad for them, but we got to investigate."

"Who's going to investigate?" Tipton asked. "We got no law. How bad is Seth hit?"

"Well, the last I heard, he was still alive, but just barely. He hasn't been able to talk to anyone yet."

"Aubrey, someone laid an ambush out at my place this morning early. They killed Lige as he was riding out. Me and Slocum found him in the road. The Beamers have declared war. That's clear."

"Killed Lige, huh? That's too bad. Lige was a good man."

"Aubrey, let's go have a drink," Tipton said.

The judge turned around on the sidewalk and headed back for the Hogneck. Tipton and Slocum rode their mounts that way. When they arrived, they dismounted and tied their horses to the rail. Then they walked inside with the judge and found a table, Tipton calling for a bottle and three glasses along the way. In a couple of minutes, Goosey brought the glasses and the bottle, and Tipton poured drinks all around.

"We got a serious situation here, Aubrey," he said.

"I've written for a U.S. marshal to come out here," said the judge.

"We can't wait for that," Tipton said. "The Beamers has come out in the open. They shot up our sheriff, broke their worthless brother out of jail, and ambushed my foreman. What will they do next? I'd say they'll attack me at my ranch. They're getting bold, Aubrey. I tell you, they're getting bold."

"If they've done all that, Carl," said Aubrey, "they're plenty brazen all right. But we can't go riding after a whole family on speculation. We've got laws, and—"

"But we got no one around here to enforce the laws. We got no choice, Aubrey. We got to take the law into our own hands."

"I can't allow that, Carl. Wait for the response to my letter. We'll have law out here again. Just be a little patient. Please."

Tipton looked over at Slocum in frustration. Slocum just shrugged. He wasn't about to voice an opinion to the face of a judge. They finished their drinks and Tipton paid. As they walked out of the saloon, Tipton was grumbling. They were moving toward the horses when Slocum put out a hand to stop Tipton. Tipton looked up to see Harman Beamer standing on the sidewalk.

"Howdy there, Mr. Tipton," said Harman. "And you, Slocum. I figured you two would come in here thinking to see my brother get his ass sent up. Funny thing about that. He got out of jail last night I heared."

"I expect you did more than just hear about it," said Tipton.

Further down the sidewalk, the judge overheard, and he stopped and turned around to watch and to listen.

"Try to prove that," said Harman.

Slocum stepped in front of Tipton. "What are you called?" he said.

"I'm Harman Beamer."

"Oh, yeah," said Slocum. "I've heard of you."

"What've you heared?"

"I've heard that you're a yellow-bellied, back-shooting chicken shit."

Harman went for his gun fast, and Slocum allowed him to get off two wild shots before he squeezed off one that ripped into Harman's face just under the nose and tore on up through his brain. Harman's head bounced grotesquely as blood spurted in front and behind. The body wobbled on its feet, then pitched forward to lay still. Slocum holstered his Colt just as the judge walked up beside Tipton.

"Did you see what happened?" said Tipton.

"I saw it," said the judge.

"Is there any reason for us to hang around here?"

"None that I know of. Beamer shot first."

"Twice," said Tipton.

"Yeah."

"Slocum," said Tipton, "let's get back to the ranch."

"Whatever you say," Slocum said.

They headed for the horses just as the girl from the Hogneck stepped out onto the sidewalk and smiled. "I haven't seen you for awhile, Carl," she said. "Why don't you come up and see me?"

Old Tipton blushed and looked down at the sidewalk.

Slocum acted as if he didn't hear anything.

"Well, Bonita," said Tipton, "I've been pretty busy, you know."

"I've heard some stuff," she said. "I think you need to relax some. Come on."

"Slocum—" said Tipton.

"I'll just be hanging around," said Slocum. "Take your time."

Tipton walked over to the door of the Hogneck where Bonita was lurking. As he approached, she took him by the arm, and they disappeared inside. Slocum did not really want to go in and get a drink. It was too early. He wondered about leaving the old man unprotected though, so he stepped inside long enough to watch the two of them disappear up the stairs. He walked over to the bar where Goosey was busy trying to look busy.

"Is there anyone else in the place?" he asked.

"Nary a soul," Goosey said.

"Thanks." Slocum walked back outside and looked across the street toward Harmony's place. Some cowboy came walking out gouging at his teeth with a toothpick. Slocum strolled on over and walked in. The place was empty of customers and probably would be until nearly lunchtime. He stepped up to the counter and waited. In a moment, Harmony appeared.

"Well, hello, cowboy," she said. "What can I get for you?"

"How about two cups of coffee?" Slocum said.

"Two cups?"

"I was kind of hoping you might sit down with me," he said.

She smiled back at him and went for two cups. She took the two cups and the coffeepot and walked to a table where she poured the cups full, set down the pot and looked at Slocum. He pulled out a chair for her, and she sat down. Then he moved around and took a chair for himself.

"Thank you," he said. "I don't much care for sitting alone."

"It's a pleasure," she said. "So you're working for old Carl?"

"Yes, ma'am," he said.

"From what I've been hearing, you're not a regular cowhand."

"Well, not exactly."

"More like a bodyguard."

"I guess you could call it that."

"And a pretty effective one, too, from what I've heard."

"It sounds like there's a lot of talk going on," Slocum said.

Harmony shrugged. "There's been a bit," she said. "Why aren't you watching out for him now?"

"There was just one Beamer in town," Slocum said. "He's not a problem anymore."

"That shot I heard—"

"Yes, ma'am."

"I see. So where did Carl go?"

"Well, I don't know if I should be telling tales," said Slocum, "but the last I saw of him, he was headed up the stairs at the Hogneck in the company of a gal they call Bonita."

He looked at Harmony to see how she would react. She looked right into Slocum's eyes and smiled. "I see," she said. "He may be old, but he's not dead."

They both laughed a little at that. Slocum drank the last of his coffee, and Harmony refilled the cup.

"Thanks," he said.

An old couple walked in just then. "Excuse me," Harmony said, and she got up to go see what they wanted. Slocum sat sipping his coffee and watched her move. Yes, he thought, she was really something.

Across the street and upstairs in the Hogneck, Bonita and old Tipton sat on the edge of the bed in one of the private rooms. She put an arm around his shoulders and kissed him on the cheek.

"I don't know what you see in an old fart like me," he said. "It must be my money."

"Darling," she said, "I won't even charge you."

He turned to look into her face, and she kissed him full on the lips. While the kiss lingered, her right hand went down to his crotch, and she felt a rise there. Letting go of the kiss, she said, "Um, Carl, you ain't so old."

"I'm feeling younger every minute," he said.

She laid him back on the bed and pulled off his boots. Then she straightened up and began to strip. Tipton watched her every move with a smile on his face. She soon tossed aside the final item of clothing and put one knee on the bed. She started to undress Tipton, taking her time, stroking and fondling each part of his body as she uncovered it. Tipton moaned with pleasure. Soon she had him naked, too, and she crawled into the bed and on top of his body. She kissed him again, and then reached down with both hands underneath her own body to find his stiff rod and fondle it.

At last, she moved the head of his cock to the waiting, wet slit between her legs. She rubbed it back and forth a few times before she slid it into place. "Ohh," she moaned, sitting up straight. Then she slid her hips back and forth slowly groaning with the pleasure and smiling down at old Carl Tipton as she did so. Carl put a hand on each of her thighs and stroked them as she rode him. At last, she began to move faster and faster, and Carl's moans grew louder and came faster, until he suddenly burst forth in one gush after another. When he was finally done, Bonita rode him for a few more strokes. Then with a loud sigh, she relaxed and fell forward to kiss him passionately.

At last, she rolled over to lay beside him. "You're wonderful, Carl," she said.

"You're pretty damn good yourself," he said. "You sure do know how to take care of an old—"

"Don't even say it," she said. "Carl, you're a robust man in the prime of your life. I never had better."

"It's good of you to say that."

"I mean it."

She turned to face him and kissed him again. Tipton turned and sat up. "Bonnie," he said, "I wish I could just stay here with you, but I've really got to get going. The way things are right now—"

"I understand, Carl. You don't have to explain anything. But don't stay away so long this time."

He turned his head to give her another kiss. "I'll try to get back real soon," he said. He stood up to get dressed, and so did she. When Tipton pulled on his boots, he stood again and reached into his pocket.

"Carl," she said, "I told you I wouldn't charge you, and I meant it."

He smiled at her and pulled out some money anyway. "You won't mind then," he said, "if I just leave you some cash to help out. Just because I want to."

He put the money on the table, kissed her one more time, put on his hat and left the room. Bonita walked over to the table and picked up the money. She counted it and saw that it was three times the amount she would have charged.

"Oh, Carl," she said. "Carl, I sure do wish you was single."

8

Goofball McGiver stood on the sidewalk watching some
men load the body of Harman Beamer to take it down the
street to the undertaker. When they had taken it inside, he
strolled casually to his horse waiting patiently at the hitch
rail. Taking the reins loose from the rail, he moved to its
side and mounted up. He turned the horse easily and
started riding out of town at a leisurely pace. As soon as
he was out of town, he looked over his shoulder to see if
anyone was watching. There was no one. He kicked his
horse wickedly in the sides and lashed at it with the long
ends of the reins, taking off as fast as he could go. When
he reached his destination, the Beamer spread, the
wretched animal was lathered up and panting. Goofball
practically leaped out of the saddle. Maw Beamer had
stepped out onto the porch.

"Goofball," she said, "what are you doing here?"

"I come bringing bad news, Maw," said Goofball.

Just then Brace stepped out to stand beside Maw.

"Well," said Maw, "what is it?"

"I'm sorry to be the one to tell you," said Goofball,
"but someone has got to."

"You ain't told me nothing yet."

"It's Harman. He was killed in town."

"Harman killed?"

"Who done it?" said Brace.

"That Slocum feller."

"Goddamn it. I knowed it. We got to kill that son of a bitch, Maw."

"Let's not have no talk of killing just yet," Maw said. "Someone's got to go into town and fetch Harman home. After the burying, we'll talk about killing."

"I'll go," Brace said.

"You ain't showing your face in town," Maw said. "Not till I say so."

"I can go back and fetch Harman out here to you if you want me to," said Goofball. "You could write me a note. If you want."

"Brace, hitch a team up to the wagon. I don't want my boy coming home slung across some saddle. Come on inside, Goofball. I'll compose that note for you."

"Yes, ma'am," Goofball said.

"And Brace, gather up what's left of the family and bring them in the house."

"All right, Maw."

As Brace headed out to get fresh horses, Maw led Goofball into the house. She found a piece of paper, a pen, and a bottle of ink. Shoving aside some dirty dishes, she put the items down on the table and sat down. Then she stared up at the ceiling for a moment. "You got to word these legal papers just right," she said. At last she dipped the pen into the ink bottle and started to write.

To whoever it is whose consarned, she wrote. *Let the barrer of this here note take posesion of the remanes of my dear boy Harman to bring him home to me for burying. Sined by Mrs. Bernice Beamer.*

She picked up the paper and waved it in the air to dry the ink. Then she handed it to Goofball. "That'll do the trick," she said.

"I'll bring him home in a flash," said Goofball.

"Don't you go to running them horses," Maw said. "Just drive easy. We'll have aplenty to do here getting ready."

"Yes'm."

Brace drove the wagon up in front of the house just as Goofball stepped out. Goofball tucked the paper into his shirtfront and mounted the wagon. Brace handed him the reins and jumped down.

"Mind what I said. Drive easy," said Maw.

"Yes'm," said Goofball. "I will. I'll go smooth and easy."

Goofball drove off and Brace headed away from the house.

"Where you going?" Maw said.

"To fetch the rest of the boys like you said."

"Well, hurry it up."

"Carl," said Slocum, as the two men rode quietly down the road back toward the ranch, "we're going to have to change our tactics."

"How do you mean?"

"I've killed three of those Beamers now," Slocum said. "They've got to be mad as hell. There's no sheriff now for them to worry about. They could try anything. How many of them are left now?"

"Well, let's see. The nearest I can figure, there's Brace and Hump and Hiram. I think there's four more brothers, or maybe cousins, I ain't sure, and then there's them two others. Hired hands or something."

"That's eight," Slocum said.

"Nine, ain't it?"

"Brace, Hump and Hiram. That's three," said Slocum. "You said four more? That'd make seven, and then the two extra. Yeah. Nine. There's nine of them. You're right."

"Nine," said Tipton. "Yeah."

"Well, nine's enough. They could mount an attack on the ranch."

"I've got more than nine hands," Tipton said. "That wouldn't be too smart of them, would it?"

"It would if they figured we weren't ready," Slocum said. "And if for sure we weren't ready, it would be a pretty good move. They could do right-smart damage to us that way."

"I guess you're right. So what do we do?"

"Let's get all your hands together and tell them what's

what," Slocum said. "Anyone who wants out, now's the time. The rest will have to be ready for anything that might happen, and that will include having guards awake and around the house all night long every night."

"We can do that. Soon as we get back."

Maw Beamer's boys all gathered at her house, all except Goofball McGiver who was still out on his chore. They sat on everything that was available, a couple of them even sitting on the floor. Maw shouted at them to shut up and pay attention. They got still.

"Now, listen to me, boys," she said. "That Slocum has went and killed another one of your brothers."

"Who?" said Hump, sitting up straight. "Who's killed?"

"Your brother Harman. Against my better judgement, he went into town today by his lonesome, and Slocum shot him down right out on the street. Goofball has took the wagon into town to fetch the body back. When he gets here, we'll have the burying. We got to do up a proper funeral. I want one of you to go out and kill some chickens and pluck them. One of you slice up a whole mess of beef. And a couple of you get busy and dig a burying hole. I want everything to be ready when Harman gets home."

"But, Maw," said Hump, "what about that Slocum?"

"Shut up about that till we're done burying your brother," Maw snapped. "Now get after it."

The boys all scattered. Maw busied herself making bread. Soon the sliced beef was brought in, and she started it cooking. Then came the chickens. She worked the rest of the day, even after Goofball returned. At last, everything was ready. Harman was brought in the house and laid out for all to see. Maw brought out her Bible and read from the Old Testament. Then she led her unholy brood in a couple of choruses of "When the Roll is Called Up Yonder." Finally, she said, "Brace, Hump, Hiram, Henley, take up the body of your fallen brother and carry it out to its final resting place."

The designated brothers took up the body and started

out the door. The others followed along slowly. When they reached the newly dug hole, they started to lower the body into it, but they dropped it at the last minute. Maw went over to the edge of the grave and looked down.

"Jump in there, Henley," she said, "and straighten up your brothers arms and legs."

Henley jumped in, stepping on the body as he did so. At last he got the job done, and he reached up with his right arm. "Give me a hand out of here," he said. Hump grabbed his hand and helped him scrabble back out of the hole. Then they all took off their hats and held them solemnly in front of themselves.

"Dear Lord," said Maw, "we're a giving you back one more of our dear sons what was taken away from us by the same evil hand what took them others. We've talked to you about it already. This is just the more reason for us to do the killing we talked on before. Be good to my boy Harman. He never done nothing wrong, and you know it. Amen. Shovel the dirt in, boys."

She turned and started walking back to the house. Hump and Hiram picked up shovels. They shoveled for awhile, then handed the shovels to Brace and Henley. Hump stepped back to lean against a fence. With the left sleeve of his shirt, he wiped sweat from his forehead. Hiram stepped over to stand beside him, wiping his face with a rag from his back pocket.

"Well, Hiram," Hump said, "Maw mentioned the killing to the Lord, so I reckon it'll be all right for us to talk about it now."

"We'll have to talk to Maw about it before we go and do anything," Hiram said.

"Oh, we'll talk to her all right," Hump said. "We'll see what she has to say. Then we'll go and do whatever has to be done. Maw ain't always just right, you know. She's getting up in years and don't think quite as clear as what she used to."

"Well, I'm going to have to think real hard and remind myself of Ike and Billy," said Hiram. "I never was too fond of ole Harman."

"You oughten speak bad about the dead," Hump said.

"I don't see no sense in lying about it just because he's gone."

"He was our brother."

"He was still a worthless shit."

Hump swung a roundhouse right that caught Hiram on the side of the head and knocked him sideways into the fresh dirt that Brace and Henley were shoveling into the grave. "Ow," shouted Hiram.

"What the hell?" said Brace.

"Son of a bitch," Hiram said.

"What was that for?" asked Oscar, another brother.

"He was talking ill of our deceased brother," said Hump.

"Is that all?" said Brace. "Hell, that ain't no call to go to hitting your own brother at a funeral."

"You mind your business," Hump said. "This here is between me and Hiram."

"Oh yeah?" said Brace, and he swung at Hump, connecting a glancing blow to Hump's chin. Hump staggered back just as Hiram got up to his feet, ducked low, and ran at him, tackling him and crashing right through the fence. A hog squealed and ran, and chickens scattered clucking and flapping their useless wings. Hump landed on his back in the nasty mud with Hiram on top of him. Quickly, Hump rolled over mashing Hiram down into the soft muck. Hiram flailed with both arms, slapping his brother on the back and doing no damage.

Brace ran to the rescue of Hiram, kicking out at Hump's ribs. His foot found its mark, but the force of the kick caused Brace's other foot to slip in the ooze, and he fell over backward and landed with a loud splash. Goofball and the other man not a member of the family stepped off to one side not wanting to become involved. Jefferson Davis Beamer and Butcher Beamer started laughing. Oscar and Henley were still shoveling dirt into the grave. Brace got up out of the mud and stepped behind Hump, reaching around his neck with both arms and choking him, trying to pull him off of Hiram.

Jefferson Davis looked at Butcher. "Hump's fighting two at once," he said.

"That ain't fair, is it?" said Butcher.

"Not hardly," said Jefferson Davis.

"You going to do anything about it?"

"Nope."

"Well, hell," said Butcher. He walked over to the graveside and reached out toward Oscar. "Give me that shovel," he said, taking the tool away from Oscar. Oscar gave it up easily, and Butcher walked toward the melee. Stepping up behind Brace he suddenly rared back with the shovel and took a swing slamming the flat of the shovel blade hard into Brace's back just between the shoulder blades.

"Yowee!" shouted Brace.

He let loose of his grip on Hump's neck and turned on his new attacker. Butcher prepared the shovel for another swing. At the same time, Hiram managed to throw Hump back off of him, and Hump fell sideways into the slime. Brace ducked low and moved toward Butcher, but he slipped in the muck and fell on his face. Butcher lowered the shovel and started to laugh. Back at the graveside, Henley had stopped shoveling and was watching the affray. He jabbed the business end of the shovel into the soft dirt, said, "Oh, hell," and started walking toward the fight. Just as he got close, Butcher turned and swung, knocking Henley back into the half-filled grave. Oscar started to laugh at that, and Butcher got up and slugged him in the jaw.

Goofball McGiver looked at his partner, Skinny Clark. "Who the hell started this fight anyhow?" he asked.

"I think Hump started it," said Skinny.

Goofball slugged Skinny. Skinny staggered back, resumed his balance and struck up a fighting stance, and the two of them began pummeling at one another, still a safe distance away from the main fight. Suddenly there was a loud blast. Everyone stopped and looked. Maw was standing there with a smoking shotgun in her hands.

"Shame, shame on all of you," she said.

"Maw," said Butcher, "we didn't—"

"Shut up!" she roared. "I don't want to hear it. I don't want to know who started it, and I don't want to know how come. Just straighten your young asses up and finish filling up that grave."

No one moved for a moment, and Maw fired the second barrel of the shotgun into the air. The boys all jumped to their feet.

"Get to it," Maw said.

She stood there while they finished the work on the grave. That included setting a wooden cross with Harman Beamer's name on it in place. When at last the job was properly finished, she said, "Now get yourselves cleaned up. You look like a bunch of fucking dirt farmers."

She turned and headed back to the house. Hump threw his arm around Hiram's shoulder. They looked at each other and smiled.

"What're we going to do, Hump?" Hiram asked.

"We'll do like Maw said," Hump answered. "We'll all get cleaned up proper, and then we'll ride out tonight and hit the Tipton ranch."

"Yeah?"

"Take torches and burn the ranch house down. Whenever Tipton and Slocum and anyone else comes running out, we'll gun them down."

"What about all them ranch hands?"

"We'll have a couple of boys watching the bunkhouse to shoot anyone who comes out of there."

"There's two women over there," said Brace, having stepped into the discussion.

"We won't shoot them," said Hump. "Not for a little while at least."

9

Arnie Tipton sat at his table alone in his run-down ranch house studying a pile of papers there in front of him. They were mostly letters written to him years before by his brother Carl. After some studying, Arnie laid out a fresh piece of paper. He took up a pen and dipped it into an ink bottle and began to write. He wrote out "Carl Tipton." He wrote slowly and carefully looking at Carl's signature as he wrote. When he had done, he studied his work. Then he tried again. Before he was finished, he had covered the sheet of paper in fake Carl Tipton signatures. The last few on the sheet looked pretty good. He was proud of himself, but he would have to practice some more before he would be ready. He leaned back in his chair and sighed heavily. Then he picked up a whiskey bottle that was sitting nearby and poured himself a drink. He downed it quickly and poured another. Then he went back to work.

Carl Tipton gathered all of his ranch hands together in front of his big house. He and Slocum were up on the porch facing the crowd. Myrtle and Jamie came out of the house to stand to one side on the porch and listen to what was going to be said. When Carl was satisfied that all were present, he called for quiet.

"Boys," he said, "I've got some things to tell you. First off, you all know that Lige was killed. It's a sad thing, and the way it was done it was a dirty, mean trick. I've got to name a new foreman, and I've decided to name

Randy Self if he's willing to take the job. What do you say, Randy?"

Randy took the hat off his head and shuffled his feet, looking down at the dirt. "Aw, gee, Mr. Tipton, I don't hardly know what to say. It's a mighty big job filling ole Lige's boots."

"You can do it, Randy, or I wouldn't have asked you. Think about it for a bit. I've got some other things to say."

"Yes, sir."

"You all know, I think," Tipton went on, "that the god-damned Beamers have went and declared war on me. They're a mean bunch. The first thing was when Brace tried to gun me in town again. Then Ike and Billy stopped me on the road with the same intentions. The last one was Harman, in town again. Slocum stopped them all. I owe him a whole lot. He's working for me as a gun hand, so if you see that you're working and he ain't, I don't want no jealousy around here about that.

"Well, our sheriff has been shot real bad, and Lige was murdered. There were no witnesses to either of them shootings, but we all know who done them, don't we?"

"The Beamers," several cowhands hollered.

Tipton held up his hands for quiet. "The Beamers done them both for sure. And now that there ain't no law around here, they're going to feel that much freer to do whatever the hell comes into their damned heads. The other thing is that Slocum has killed three of them. So it looks to me, and to Slocum as well, that the war is on for sure. So what I called all of you together here for is this. You all hired on to be cowhands. If you don't want no part in this coming war, I won't blame you if you decide to quit. I'll pay you off, and I'll give you a little bonus. You can ride out of here with no hard feelings. So if you want out, now's the time to say so."

He turned his back and walked to the door, standing there in silence for a time. There was some muttering among the hands. Slocum lit a cigar and noticed that the ladies were talking low to one another. Finally, Tipton turned back around and stepped out to the front of the porch.

"Well?" he bellowed.

No one said anything. No one stepped forward.

"What do you say?"

Randy Self took a step forward and looked up at Tipton. "Mr. Tipton," he said, "there ain't a one going to quit on you, and, well, I'll take that foreman's job."

"Good," said Tipton. "The next thing I'm going to do is to ask Slocum to talk to you. He's the gunman around here, and he's going to take charge as long as this damned war keeps on. Slocum?"

Slocum stood up slowly and walked to the front of the porch. At the same time, Tipton turned away and found himself a chair.

"Men," said Slocum, "from now on go armed. Wear your revolvers and carry your rifles. If anyone goes out to the pasture or out fixing fence, anything like that, go in twos at least. I don't want no one getting caught out alone. The same things goes for any trips you might make into town. At least two of you go together. You got that, Randy?"

"Yes, sir," Randy said. "I'll see to it."

"All right. I want two men down there at the main gate watching for any sign of trouble. I want two men at the house around the clock. Randy, you can work out the schedules. And I want at least a couple of men riding fence constant, patrolling the borders of this ranch. Now if any of you see any sign of trouble, and it's just the two of you, hightail it back here to let the rest know what's up. I don't want two men trying to fight it out with ten Beamers. Well, I reckon that's about all I got to say."

"Take over, Randy!" Tipton shouted.

The cowhands gathered around Randy to see what he had to say, and he immediately began making assignments to follow the instructions Slocum had given. In almost no time, two cowhands with rifles and revolvers mounted up and headed for the main gate. Two more positioned themselves there at the house, and four men went out in two different directions to begin the fence riding. Slocum pulled a chair up next to Tipton and sat down, puffing his cigar.

"Well, Slocum," said Tipton, "what do you think?"

"We'll handle them all right, Carl," Slocum said. "You got too many men here for us to lose."

"Yeah, but I can't live here the rest of my life like a goddamned prisoner."

"Didn't the judge say that he'd wrote a letter to the U.S. marshal?"

"Yeah, but—"

"We can hold out till the marshal gets here. Then all we have to do is to just accuse the Beamers of those killings. We've got Brace already on attempted murder and jailbreaking. It likely won't take much to set them crazy bastards off. With the U.S. marshal on our side, we can go wipe them out if we have to."

"I guess so," Tipton said.

The ladies had walked up close behind the two chairs where Tipton and Slocum were sitting and had been listening to the conversation.

"Carl," said Myrtle, "you pay attention to what Slocum's saying. It makes good sense."

"Yes, Daddy," said Jamie. "After all, it's what you're paying him for, isn't it?"

"Yeah," Tipton said. "You're right. All of you."

Ace and Trotter were riding herd later that evening. The sun was about to go down beyond the horizon. The cattle were a bit restless, but the two hands were able to keep them calm with no trouble. Suddenly a group of riders appeared not too far away.

"Hey, Trotter," said Ace. "See that?"

"Beamers?" said Trotter.

"Who else?"

"What do we do?"

"Just what Slocum said. We ride like hell for help."

One of the riders in the far group raised a rifle to his shoulder and fired a shot. It was a long shot, but it hit its mark. Ace jerked and pitched forward, falling from his saddle. His horse nickered and bolted.

"Ace," said Trotter. He started to dismount, but a second shot sounded, and Trotter felt it bite his left shoulder. He looked frantically in the direction of the gang of riders and saw that they were riding toward him. He looked down at Ace, wondering if he were dead or alive. He looked back at the riders coming fast. With his right hand, he pulled his revolver and fired off a couple of quick shots. He saw a horse stumble and fall, throwing its rider. Then he kicked hard at his own horse's sides and rode fast for the ranch house.

Hump Beamer called a halt and rode over to the side of his fallen brother, Butcher. Butcher got slowly up to his feet. "Goddamn," he said.

"You hurt?" said Hump.

"No, but my goddamn horse sure as hell is."

"He looks like he's killed to me," Hump said.

"Well, goddamn it, what am I going to ride on?"

"Shit," said Hump. "Get up behind Skinny, but you two can't ride on with the rest of us double like that. Just go on back to the house."

"Ah, damn it," said Butcher.

"Why me?" said Skinny.

"Because I said so, and I'm the oldest," Hump said. "Now just get on and do it."

Skinny rode his horse over close to Butcher, and Butcher climbed on the back still grumbling. Skinny did not bother to turn his horse around just yet. He and Butcher sat there watching the others.

"All right, the rest of you, come on and follow me," Hump said, and he started to ride toward the ranch house of the Tipton spread. Skinny and Butcher watched them go.

"I don't want to go on back home," said Butcher. "Not just on account of losing my damn horse."

"Well, what'll we do?" said Skinny.

"Say, where's the horse of that ole boy we shot down?"

"It's got to be around here somewheres."

"Let's ride around a little bit and see can we spot it."

"All right."

Skinny rode his horse forward toward the cattle herd, toward the place where Ace was when he was shot. The cattle stirred uneasily. Skinny kept going right toward them.

"Hey," said Butcher. "Over there."

He pointed off to his right, and Skinny turned his head to look.

"What is it?" he said.

"Look there on the ground. There's that one we shot."

Skinny spotted the body on the ground. He turned his horse to ride over to it. When they got there, he stopped, and Butcher jumped down off the horse. He unbuckled Ace's gun belt and jerked it loose from the body, throwing it over his shoulder. Then he rummaged through all of the pockets, taking any money he found. He also took a pocket-knife. Last of all, he pulled the boots off the dead feet. Tucking the boots into the saddle-bags on Skinny's horse, he climbed back on.

"That horse's got to be around here somewhere," he said.

"Loose like that and still saddled. Hell," said Skinny, "he might've gone straight on back to the corral."

"He might," said Butcher, "but he might could still be around. Let's look some more."

They rode to the rear of the cattle herd. Skinny was about to turn his horse to ride around to the other side when Butcher stopped him. There, a little further off to his right, stood the loose horse, grazing contentedly.

"Ride up to him real easy," Butcher said. "Don't take no chances of scaring him off."

"I can catch a horse," said Skinny. He eased his own mount forward edging closer to the loose Tipton horse. It raised its head nickered, then moved and nickered, then moved a few feet farther away.

"Go easy, I said."

"Hush up, Butcher."

Skinny stopped his horse, and they sat there for a couple of minutes. Then he urged it forward again, slowly. The loose horse kept grazing. Skinny eased up close. Both men talked soft to the horse. Skinny scooched in close beside it and reached down for the reins. He got hold of one. "Hot damn," said Butcher, sliding off the back end of Skinny's horse. He ran around and climbed up onto the other horse, catching up the reins.

"I reckon it's too late to catch up to Hump and them," he said.

"I'd say so."

"Well, then," said Butcher, "let's just see how many of these damned Tipton cows we can drive over onto our own range."

"That suits me," said Skinny.

They took loose their ropes and began riding around the herd swinging them and calling out to the cattle. The already high-strung beasts were not hard to get moving. A few straggled off to either side, but the majority of the herd headed out in the direction the two thieves wanted.

"Yeah," hollered Butcher. "Keep them moving."

"Woo ha!" shouted Skinny. "Get along there. Get along."

Moving along at a slow run, some of the cattle trampled over the body of Ace. They kept going. Butcher suddenly had a thought, an unusual occurrence for him. He called out at the top of his lungs to Skinny, "Hey, there's a fence up yonder."

"I'll cut it," shouted Skinny, spurring his horse ahead. He had soon disappeared from Butcher's view, and Butcher did what he could to keep the herd moving along at a steady pace. He lost a few more, especially from the side of the herd that Skinny had been riding.

"Yow. Yow," he shouted. A big bull turned and ran out of the herd, and Butcher rode to head him off. The bull turned in the nick of time, just bashing his side into the side of Butcher's mount. The bull turned back into the herd, but Butcher's horse stumbled and almost fell down, Butcher sliding halfway out of the saddle.

"Hell damn!" he shouted, as he fought to regain his seat. "Son of a bitch," he said, drawing out his six-gun and riding up alongside the bull. He cocked the revolver and fired into the bull's side. He fired again. The bull

stumbled over its front knees and crashed into the ground.
The rest of the herd kept moving, but they moved faster
than ever now. Butcher knew that the fence was dead
ahead. He kept the herd moving fast, hoping that Skinny
had done his job. Hell, he thought, even if he ain't, it ain't
no skin off me. They ain't my damn cows.

When the bawling herd reached the fence, Skinny had
already removed a long section of the vicious barbed wire,
and the cattle moved through the fence with no problem.
Once the last one was through, Butcher stopped riding so
hard. He had them where he wanted them. Skinny rode
up beside him. They sat at the rear of the herd and
watched them run.

"Where they going to wind up?" Skinny asked.

"Damned if I know," said Butcher. "They might run
right up onto the house if they keep going like that."

"What'll your maw say?"

"I don't think she'll mind too much," Butcher said.
"You know that beef we had at Harman's funeral?"

"Yeah."

"Was it good?"

"It was pretty damn good."

"Well, hell, it was Tipton beef."

10

Trotter made it to the ranch house, but he was about to fall out of the saddle. Charlie Hope and another cowhand were guarding the house. Everyone but the guards on duty had gone to bed. The house was dark. Charlie came running when he heard the horse. As he got close, he thought that he could recognize the rider in the dark, but he also thought that something looked wrong.

"Trotter?" he said. "That you?"

"Charlie," said Trotter. "Yeah, it's me."

Charlie ran on over to the horse. He saw that Trotter was sagging in the saddle. He leaned his rifle against the hitch rail and reached up to give Trotter a hand.

"Charlie," said Trotter. "Wake everyone up. They're coming. They killed Ace. Shot me. I knocked down one of their horses and slowed them up a little, but they won't be far behind."

"Joe," yelled Charlie, as he helped Trotter down. "Joe. Come a running."

Trotter got his feet on the ground and an arm around Charlie's shoulder. They were moving toward the porch when Joe came around a corner of the house.

"What is it?" he said.

"Trotter's been shot. Ace is killed. The Beamers is on the way here. Wake everyone up."

Joe ran up on the porch and began pounding on the door. Slocum was there in a flash, and old Tipton was not far behind. Joe gave a quick explanation of what was going on, and Tipton had Charlie take the wounded Trotter into the house. Then he sent Joe scurrying to the bunkhouse to wake up the whole crew. In a short time, everyone was gathered around the house fully armed. Myrtle and Jamie were tending to Trotter's wound inside. Quickly, Slocum spotted men around he house and at strategic locations in the yard. He told them to be ready. "Those bastards mean business," he said.

Out on the range, Hump Beamer led his riotous gang toward the ranch house at breakneck speed. When they got close, he slowed them down. Finally he stopped. He sat still in the saddle for a moment studying the situation. At last he spoke in a low voice, but loud enough for all to hear. "It looks quiet," he said. "Everyone's gone to bed. That's good. We'll ride in real close, and you Hiram and you Jeff get off your horses and go right up to the house and start it on fire. Then run back to your horses and join up with the rest of us. We'll let the fire get going. That'll make the folks inside come a running out, and when they do, we'll cut loose on them. Kill everyone you can."

"Except the women," said Brace. He had an evil leer on his face.

"Yeah," said Hump. "Save the women if you can. We'll kill them later."

"When we're all done with them," said Brace.

"All right now," said Hump. "Let's get our minds on our business. Everyone know what to do?"

"Hell, yes," Brace said. "We're raring to go."

"Let's do it then," said Hump. "Hiram, Jeff, get a move on."

Hiram and Jeff rode in yet closer before they dismounted. They stood still for a moment looking at the house. Then they looked at one another.

"You got matches?" Hiram asked.

"Yeah. You?"

"Yeah."

"Well then," said Jefferson Davis Beamer, "let's go do it."

"Well," Hiram stammered, "what'll we use to start the fire with?"

"What do you mean?"

"You can't just hold a match to a house and start it a burning, can you?"

"No, you silly shit. What you do is you gather up some trash. You know, some dry grass and such, and you pile it against the side of the house and set it on fire."

"Oh. Say, there's a haystack over yonder."

"Good idea. Let's go get us each a handful of that hay."

They crouched down and started moving stealthily toward the haystack. They had made it about halfway when a shot was fired. Hiram yelped fearfully and slapped a hand to the side of his head.

"Someone's went and shot my left ear off," he yowled.

"Let's get out of here," said Jefferson Davis.

The two of them turned to run for their horses. Another shot was fired that ripped the heel off of Jefferson Davis's right boot. Jefferson Davis was running lopsided. He stumbled and rolled in the ground. Terrified, he scrambled to his feet and continued to run with a stupid-looking limp. More shots sounded as the two reached their horses. Mounting hurriedly, they rode back to where Hump and the others waited.

"Let's get out of here," Jefferson Davis hollered.

"My fucking ear's shot off," whimpered Hiram.

"Come on," Hump said, turning his horse. "The bastards was laying for us."

"That's a dirty damn trick," said Brace.

The entire gang turned their horses and headed back across the open range the way they had come. A few shots were fired from behind them, but none of them found a mark.

"I'm bleeding to death," Hiram roared.

"Well, shut up and ride," said Hump.

Slocum stepped down off the porch. He surveyed the situation as he holstered his Colt. "They're gone, boys," he called. "Come on out." The cowhands all appeared in the yard around Slocum.

"Should we go after them?" Randy Self asked.

"No. It wouldn't do any good in this dark," Slocum said. "You did good. All of you. Those of you that got rousted out of bed, go on back. Those of you that was on guard duty get back to your posts. Randy, you'll have to replace Ace and Trotter. And whoever you pick, tell them to watch out. We don't want anyone else shot up if we can avoid it."

"Yes sir, Slocum," Randy said.

Slocum turned and walked back up onto the porch. He sat down heavily in a chair. Carl Tipton sat down next to him.

"Good job, Slocum," he said. "You want a drink?"

"I'll take one," said Slocum.

Tipton got up and went into the house. A moment later he reappeared with a bottle and two glasses. He sat down again and poured the glasses full, handing one to Slocum.

"Thanks," Slocum said.

"Hell," said Tipton, "you earned it. That and more."

They finished off the first glass, and Tipton poured them both refills.

"You've got good taste in whiskey," Slocum said. "That's how come I'm hanging around here."

Tipton chuckled. "So what do we do from here?" he asked. "Attack the Beamers at their place and wipe them out?"

"That's what I feel like doing," Slocum said, "but I don't believe it would look very good. You remember what the judge said."

"Wait for the U.S. marshal," said Tipton, disgust sounding in his voice.

"How long can we hold out here at the ranch without anyone going into town for anything?"

"Well, let's see now," said Tipton. "I think we could last a week. Maybe more. We've got plenty of grub and coffee. Tobacco. I can't think what else we need to go to town for."

"Ammunition?" Slocum asked.

"Got enough to finish off a war with," Tipton said.

"All right then," said Slocum. "Let's just lay low, keep our guards out. See if they try to pull anything else. As long as they're attacking us, we're in the clear."

"Okay," said Tipton. "Well, I've got to go on back to bed. I'm getting too old for this."

Slocum thought about Tipton's turn in town with Bonita. "I don't think you're acting none too old," he said.

"Ha. You want me to leave this bottle with you?"

Slocum reached out and took it. "Thanks," he said. Tipton went on in the house. Slocum took out a cigar and lit it. Then he sipped at his second drink until he finished it and poured himself another. He was sitting there smoking and sipping when he heard the door open behind him. He twisted his head and saw Jamie come out onto the porch.

"How's the patient?" he asked.

"He'll be all right," Jamie said. "He took a shot in the shoulder, so he won't be much good for anything for a spell, but it'll mend."

"I'm glad to hear it," said Slocum. "You want a drink? Carl left the bottle with me."

"After a day like today," she said, "that sounds pretty good. I'll just go get me a glass."

She went into the house but was back in a jiffy, handing the glass to Slocum. He poured it full and gave it back to her. She sat down where Carl had been and sipped the drink.

"Ah," she said. "That's just what I needed."

"Yeah," said Slocum. "Me, too."

"Slocum?" she said.

He looked at her. "Yes?"

"I was pretty smart with you that first day you were here," she said. "I want to apologize for that."

"Oh, there's no apology called for," he said.

"I just want you to know that I'm glad you're here."

"Thanks."

She finished her drink and held the glass out toward Slocum. He gave her a curious look. "You sure you want another one?" he asked.

"Of course," she said.

He poured the glass full a second time, and she took a long sip. Even in the darkness, he could tell that her face was flushed, and he had already taken note of the fact that her voice was slightly slurred. He was having mixed feelings about this little encounter. He thought again about Carl and Myrtle. What would they think if they found out that he was taking advantage of their daughter? But then, Jamie was a grown woman. She had her own mind. And just now, in the dim light of the night, she looked especially appealing. He was trying to decide what to say next when she saved him the trouble.

"Slocum," she said, leaning in close to him, "kiss me."

He leaned over and their lips met. Tenderly at first, then the kiss became more passionate with tongues probing and dueling with each other. At last they broke away. Slocum leaned back in his chair.

"Jamie," he said, "this shouldn't go any further."

"I know you'll ride away when this is all over," she said. "You don't have to worry about hurting me."

"Your folks trust me," he said.

"I'm a grown woman," she said. "And everyone is asleep."

"Not those two cowhands lurking around the house here," he said.

"Oh," she said. "Well, then, you go on in to your room, and I'll be there in a few minutes."

Slocum tried to think of another reason that he should put a stop to this before it was too late, but nothing would come into his mind. He stood up, taking his glass and the whiskey bottle. "Well," he said, "I'll just say good night to you then. I'll be going to my room."

As he moved to the door, she smiled and said, "Good night, Slocum."

Slocum was undressed and sitting on the edge of the bed with a drink in his hand when the door opened and Jamie slipped in. She closed the door behind herself quietly. She looked at him and smiled. A bit of moonlight was slightly illuminating the otherwise dark room. As she walked across the room, she took off one piece of clothing after another and dropped them to the floor. When she reached the bed, she was naked. She put one knee on the bed on each side of Slocum's legs and sat down straddling his thighs. With her arms tight around him, she kissed him furiously on the mouth. Slocum's hands stroked her bare back. She leaned into him until he fell over backwards onto the bed. Already he could feel his tool start to rise.

"Oh, Slocum," she said, for she could feel it as well.

She crawled off of him and moved to the middle of the bed, getting onto her hands and knees. She turned her head to give him a coy look. "Do you want to take me from behind?" she said.

"Just like a stallion and mare," he said.

He crawled in behind her and, on his knees, moved in close. Taking his engorged cock in his hand, he felt around for her waiting slit, and he rubbed the head of his member up and down until it was dripping wet with desire. Then he found just the right spot, and he thrust forward, deep into her lusciousness.

"Oh," she said. "Oh. Oh. Oh."

Slocum thrust in and pulled out again and again. Faster and faster. He pounded himself against her round, bare buttocks with loud slapping sounds.

"Oh. Oh. Oh," she said.

He thought that he could finish quickly like this, but that wouldn't be fair to her, so he stopped suddenly all the way in. He kept still, savoring the pleasure of the feeling inside her.

"Oh, that's good," she said.

Slocum slowly slipped out. "Why don't you get on top and ride me?" he said.

"Oh, yeah."

Slocum lay down on his back, his rigid tool standing almost straight up. She looked at it with delight in her eyes. Reaching out, she took hold of the slimy rod, then swung one leg over as if she were mounting a horse. Astraddle of him, she poked around with his rod until she found her own wet hole. Then she slid down all the way.

"Ah, my God," she said.

She started to rock back and forth, slowly at first, moaning and groaning with pleasure at each movement. "Oh, yeah. Oh, yeah," she said. Her motions became faster and faster yet. At last she was humping furiously, moving as fast as she could. "Oh. Oh. Oh." Slocum knew that he could not last much longer. He was relieved when she moaned out long and loud, and he knew that she was coming. He, too, was just about finished. He felt the building pressure in his heavy balls, and then he felt the sudden release gush over and over, shooting her full of his thick juices. Finally she stopped moving. She took a few deep breaths, and then she allowed herself to fall forward, pressing her breasts to his chest, pressing her lips to his.

"Slocum," she said, "I am glad you're here."

11

Maw slapped Butcher hard across the face. "Ow, Maw, what was that for? Didn't I do good?"

"You done just fine, boy," said Maw. "The only thing is that I never told you to steal no cattle. I'm the one around here supposed to do the thinking. From now on you remember that."

"But, Maw, Hump and them rode off and left us, and then there was all them cows, and we had to come back home anyhow, so we just thought we'd bring them along."

Maw put her arms around Butcher and began petting his head. "It's all right now," she said. "If you'd have asked me, likely I'd have told you to go on ahead and do it. You done good. It's just that you didn't ask me. That's all."

"It won't happen again, Maw."

"See that it don't."

Across the room Skinny Clark lurked in as dark a shadow as he could find. He was hoping that Maw's rage didn't turn on him. He was relieved when she changed the subject.

"You boys sit down at the table now, and I'll fetch you some coffee and something to eat."

Skinny and Butcher took places at the table, and Maw poured them some coffee. Then she put a platter of bread on the table and went for something else. They heard horses ride up outside. Maw went to the door and opened it to see Hump and the rest of her brood dismounting.

"Take care of the horses and then come on in," she said.

"Maw, my ear's been shot off. I'm bleeding to death," Hiram whimpered.

"I said take care of your horses and then come on in," Maw bellowed. "I'll look at it then."

"Aw, Maw," whined Hiram, but he started leading the horse toward the corral with the rest of the boys. Maw slammed the door and went back to her work. She sliced off a chunk of brisket and put it on the table for Butcher and Skinny. Butcher took a knife to it. The two were still greedily stuffing their mouths with meat and bread and slurping coffee when Hump and the rest came in.

"Shut the door," Maw said. "You wasn't born in no barn, and I ought to know."

Oscar, the last one in, shut the door. Hump was about to sit down, but Maw stopped him. "You wasn't told to sit down," she said. Hump stood back up and backed away from the table. "You all line up here in a straight line," Maw said. They all lined up next to Hump. Maw went to the end of the line and slapped Oscar across the face.

"Maw, what—"

"Shut up," she said.

She stepped to the next one and did the same. When she came to Hiram she looked at the bloody side of his head.

"You've done got yours," she said. The next in line was Goofball McGiver. "You deserve it as much as any, but you ain't mine to slap," she said. She continued slapping her way down the line until she came to Hump. She stopped and looked him hard in the face.

"Maw," he said, "What's this—"

She drew back and slapped him hard, harder than she had slapped any of the others. Before he had time to react to the first slap, she smacked him again on the other cheek, and then again and again.

"You're the oldest, Hump," she said. "You'd ought to know better. You don't go off on your own. You come to me if you think you got a plan. Ask me about it. Do you understand me? Well, do you?"

"Yes, Maw," said Hump. "But we didn't think that you was going to have us do anything right away. We thought the time was right and—"

"Was the time right?" she said.

"Well—"

"What did you accomplish?"

"Well, they was waiting for us, and—"

"And you got one horse killed and your brother's ear shot off. You see what happens when you act on your own?"

"Yes, Maw."

"Now, I want you to listen to me. All of you." She turned on Butcher and Skinny who were still stuffing their mouths. "I said all of you. Put that down and listen." The two laid down the food that was in their hands and stopped chewing, looking at Maw intently. "From now on, no one does anything that I ain't told you to do. I mean you two as well, you Skinny and Goofball. You ain't my own boys, but as long as you're hanging around here, you do what I say. You got that?"

"Yes, ma'am," Skinny said.

"Yes'm," said Goofball.

"Now," she said, "the only ones that done any good tonight was the two you left behind. Butcher and Skinny brought home a bunch of Tipton's beef." She grinned, and the boys relaxed. She was over her rage. "Well," she went on, "they used to be Tipton's beef. Now all you boys find yourself a place to perch, and I'll get you something to eat."

"Maw," said Hiram, "what about my ear?"

"Oh, hell," she said, "it's quit bleeding. It's all scabbed up. When you've et you can wash it off."

"But it's shot off."

"It ain't shot off," she said. "It's just shot in two. It looks to me like both pieces is still hanging onto the side of your head. Now do like I said and shut up about it."

• • •

"A big section of fence was cut out last night, and a whole mess of cattle was drove out going toward the Beamer's place," Randy Self said.

"Damn," said Tipton.

They had just finished breakfast when Randy had knocked on the door. Tipton and Slocum each still had a coffee cup in their hands and were still sitting at the table. Myrtle and Jamie were in the kitchen cleaning up, but when Jamie heard Randy talking, she stepped through the door to listen. In another moment, Myrtle appeared in the doorway wiping her hands on a towel.

"You want us to go after them?" said Randy.

"Hell, yes," Tipton said. "I'll ride with you."

"I don't advise it," said Slocum. "Not just yet."

"What?" said Tipton, turning to face Slocum. "Why the hell not?"

"It looks to me like that attack on the house last night might've been just to keep our attention here while they drove off them cows. If that's the case, they're liable to be laying in wait for us."

"But we outnumber the bastards," said Tipton.

"We're still better off getting them over here on your own range," said Slocum. "We want to be in the clear when that marshal shows up. They won't do much with the cattle for a few days anyhow."

"So what do we do?" Tipton said. "Just sit here on our thumbs?"

"Let's you and me and a couple of the boys take a ride into town and have a talk with the judge," Slocum said. "At least we can get clear with the judge before we do anything else."

"All right," said Tipton. "Let's go get it over with."

Soon Slocum, Tipton, Charlie Hope, and Joe rode into Breakneck. They tied their horses in front of the judge's office and went inside. Judge Aubrey Lennon stood up as they walked in and shook hands with Carl Tipton.

"Hello, Carl," he said. "What brings you in here?"

"Well, you notice I come in force," said Tipton.

"That's just in case any of them damn Beamers is lurking around on the road or in town."

"Can't say I blame you for that," said the judge. "I got some news for you. Good and bad."

"What's the good news?" said Tipton.

"The sheriff's come around. He'll be down for a spell yet, but he's talking. It was Hump Beamer who shot him. He was looking at him right in the face when it happened."

"I knew it," said Tipton.

"Well, I think we all did," said Lennon, "but now we got proof."

"What's the bad news?" Slocum said.

The judge looked over at Slocum with a long face. "I got an answer to my wire," he said. "We can't have a U.S. marshal here for another couple of weeks."

"Anything can happen in that time," Slocum said.

"Yeah," the judge agreed.

"Listen here, Aubrey," Tipton said. "The Beamers attacked my house last night. We were ready for them, and drove them off without anyone getting hurt. But about the same time that was happening, some of them stole a herd of my cattle and killed Ace. They shot up Trotter, too. He managed to get back to the ranch house and warn us. Aubrey, we got to do something."

The judge paced the floor and stroked his chin whiskers for a moment. Then he turned to face Tipton again.

"I got me an idea," he said. "We got the goods on Brace for his attempted murder on you and for escaping jail. And now we got the goods on Hump for shooting the sheriff and breaking Brace out of jail. I'll put out a notice that they're wanted men. That'll make them fair game for anyone bold enough to shoot at them."

"What about the rest of them?" Tipton said.

"My guess is that if anyone should go after Brace and Hump, the others will stand up for them. If they were to get shot down in the process, well, that's just the way it is."

"How soon can you get that done?" Slocum asked.

"If you men want to hang around town for a while, I'll have it all taken care of."

"You can find us over at the Hogneck," Tipton said. "Let's go, boys."

They walked out of Lennon's office and straight across to the Hogneck. Tipton called for a bottle and four glasses and led the way to an empty table where they all sat down. In a couple of minutes, Goosey brought the bottle and glasses, and Tipton paid him. Then he poured a round of drinks.

"Thanks, Mr. Tipton," said Joe.

"Yeah," said Charlie. "Thank you."

"Drink up," said Tipton.

Slocum looked around and noted with pleasure that Bonita was nowhere to be seen. These two cowhands likely knew all about the old man's affair, but he still did not really want to witness any more of it if he didn't have to. He picked up his drink and took a sip. It was really a little early in the day for him. Still, the whiskey was good.

"I wish Aubrey would hurry it up with that business," Tipton said. "I don't like being away from the ranch while all this is still up in the air."

"It'll be all right," Slocum said. "Randy's got a good handle on things. He's got the guards out in all the right places, and there ain't no cows on that range where the Beamers hit before."

"They could hit somewhere else," Tipton said.

"Not likely," said Slocum. "Where they hit was the easiest place for them to drive the cows on over to their place. I think we'll be all right for a spell."

"They're a bunch of chickenshits," said Tipton, "and that's for sure."

"We'll take care of them," said Slocum, "just as soon as that judge gets that paperwork done."

"We're all ready to go," said Joe.

"Yeah," said Charlie. "You know we're all with you."

"I know that, boys," said Tipton, "and I thank you for it."

With four men drinking, the bottle was soon empty, and Tipton called out to Goosey for another. Goosey brought it right away, and Tipton paid again. Again, he poured the rounds.

"Goosey," he said, "you seen any Beamers around town this morning?"

"No, sir," said Goosey. "Ain't seen any of them for a few days. Not since Slocum killed that one out in the street."

"Okay," said Tipton. "Thanks."

"Why don't you try to relax a little, Carl," Slocum said. "We're fixing to be in control here."

"I guess you're right about that, Slocum, but there's killing to be done. Lots of killing."

"That's my job," said Slocum.

They had just about finished the second bottle when Aubrey Lennon came walking in with a stack of papers. He walked straight to the table where Slocum and the others were sitting, and he tossed the papers down in front of Tipton. They were wanted posters offering a reward of $100 each for the capture of Brace Beamer and Hump Beamer for attempted murder and for jailbreaking.

"Hump didn't break jail," said Tipton.

"He aided in it," said the judge.

"Oh. Well, I guess that's right."

"I just wish we had a witness to the killing of Lige and of Ace," Lennon said.

"Whichever one of them did both of those killings," said Slocum, "we'll get them. We'll get them all."

"Sit down and have a drink with us, Aubrey," said Tipton. "We might just as well finish off this bottle before we head back."

"Don't mind if I do," said the judge, and he pulled out a chair to sit down. Tipton called out to Goosey, "Bring another glass around."

Goosey brought the glass, and Tipton poured it full.

"Thanks, Carl," said the judge. He lifted the glass and took a drink. "So now that we have these dodgers out," he said, "what do you plan to do?"

Tipton looked at Slocum for an answer to that one.

"Well," Slocum said, "I guess we'll just ride on over

to the Beamer's place in force and ask them to kindly
hand over these two."

"Ha," snorted Tipton. "That'll never happen."

"That's the point, ain't it?"

Out at Arnie Tipton's ranch, Arnie was out back of the
house with a rifle. He had carefully placed bottles along
a fence rail some yards distant. Lifting the rifle to his
shoulder, he took careful aim and fired. One bottle shattered. He fired a second shot and missed.

"Damn," he said.

He cranked another shell into the chamber, aimed again
and fired, shattering another bottle. Then another and another. Soon all of the bottles were broken. He lowered the
rifle and sighed long and loud. Then he turned and walked
back into his house.

12

Slocum rode at the head of a large group of Tipton's cowhands right onto the Beamer spread and up to the house. Maw Beamer came out onto the porch with her shotgun in her hands as the riders came to a halt.

"What do you want here?" she demanded.

"We came for Hump and Brace," said Slocum. He produced one of the bills the judge had given him. "They're both wanted by the law."

"They ain't here," Maw said. "Now get off my property."

"I don't think we can take your word for that," Slocum said. "We'd better have a look through your house."

"The first one of you that gets off his horse is going to get a bellyful of shot," Maw said. "Get out of here."

Randy Self was riding next to Slocum. Looking at Maw, he spoke low to Slocum.

"What are we going to do?" he said. "We can't shoot a woman, and I think she means business with that scattergun."

"Let's ride off," said Slocum. Then he raised his voice to Maw. "We'll be back for them," he said. "They're going to face the music."

"Just what are they wanted for?" Maw said.

"Brace was already convicted," said Slocum. "You know that. You were at the trial. Then Hump went and broke him out of jail and shot the sheriff."

"What makes you think Hump done that?"

"The sheriff ain't dead," said Slocum. "He finally came around, and he named Hump as the one that shot him. I think you'd best turn them over."

"To hell with what you think and to hell with you," Maw said. She pointed the shotgun menacingly at Slocum. "Now get out of here."

Slocum turned his big Appaloosa and started riding away from the house. The other riders followed him. He judged when he was beyond the range of the shotgun. Then he stopped and turned back to face the house again. Then he pulled the Winchester out of the boot and cranked a shell into the chamber. The other cowhands did the same. Maw saw what they were doing.

"Brace," she called out. "Get your guns."

She went into the house and slammed the door. Almost instantly a front window was smashed from inside the house and a rifle barrel appeared.

"Take cover, boys," Slocum shouted. "They're in there."

Slocum and the Tipton hands all dismounted and searched out cover. There was a clump of trees nearby, and some of them went there. There was trash all over the yard in front of the house: a broken-down wagon, some barrels, and some old crates. Men ducked behind all of them. Slocum and Randy found cover behind the wagon. The rifle at the window had started firing, and Slocum and the Tipton hands returned fire.

Inside the house, Maw and four of her boys had grabbed rifles and were jockeying for positions at the windows. Brace was firing from the broken window. Hiram had opened the door a crack and was firing from there. Oscar went to the other window in the front of the house and smashed it.

"Henley," Maw said, "take that side window. You can see them from there."

Henley moved quickly to the side window and smashed it out, poking his rifle barrel out and firing from there. Maw went out the back door with her rifle and edged up to a corner of the house to peer around. She caught sight of a cowboy lurking behind a barrel. Raising the rifle to her shoulder, she took aim and fired. The cowboy yelped and fell to the ground.

"Behind the house," Slocum shouted, and he and Randy both aimed their rifles and fired a barrage of shots. Maw shrieked, hit in the shoulder. She dropped the rifle, and another shot hit her in the chest. Before her body could fall to the ground, she was hit three more times.

Inside the house, at the side window, Henley took a bullet through the side of his head. He dropped to the floor. About that same time, Hiram was hit by a half dozen shots. He staggered back, jerking convulsively, then fell hard in the middle of the floor. Brace, terrified, looked over at Oscar, who was still firing.

"Oscar," he shouted. "We got to get out of here. They're killing us."

Oscar stepped aside from the window and looked around. He saw Hiram and Henley both on the floor. "Where's Maw?" he said.

"Hell," said Brace. "I don't know. Let's get out of here."

Brace ran to the back door with Oscar on his heels. He reached for the door handle, and Oscar said, "Careful, Brace. There might be some of them back there."

"I don't think so," Brace said. He opened the door and eased out cautiously. Looking around, he saw no one. No shots came at them, although shots were still being fired at the house from out front.

"Come on," he said.

Oscar followed him out. Holding their guns ready, they looked around in all directions. Then Oscar noticed something at the far corner of the house.

"Brace," he said. "Looky there."

Brace looked and saw what appeared to be part of Maw's dress. He ran over and looked around the corner. He jumped back quickly, a look of horror on his face. Oscar noted the look. "What is it?" he said.

"It's Maw," said Brace. "She's dead."

"Let's get out of here," said Oscar.

They ran into the woods behind the house, moving into deep underbrush. Out front, Slocum called out for the Tipton riders to cease firing. It took several calls, but they finally stopped. Everything was quiet. They waited a moment. Then Randy spoke up.

"You think we got them all?" he said.

"They've stopped shooting," said Slocum. "They're either dead or of out of bullets. Let's find out."

Slocum stood up behind the wagon and started walking toward the house. A cowboy to his far right got up and started moving in, and another on his far left did the same. They approached the house slowly and cautiously, holding their rifles ready. No shots were fired. When Slocum reached the front door, he toed it open. Stepping inside quickly, he saws the bodies of Hiram and Henley. There was no one else. The other two cowboys stepped in behind him.

"Just two?" said one of the hands.

"There was more than that," Slocum said, and he looked at the open back door. Walking across the room, he stepped out, still ready for anything, but nothing happened. He walked out a bit farther and looked around. By then the rest of the Tipton crew had come up to the house. Randy Self had walked around the house on the outside.

"Hey, Slocum," Randy said.

"What is it?"

"Over here."

Slocum walked toward the corner of the house where Randy waited, and he saw the body of the old woman.

"Damn," he said.

"I guess we killed her," said Randy.

"Not before she killed one of our boys," Slocum said. "It's pretty clear where these Beamers got their dispositions."

"Yeah," Randy said. "I guess you're right about that."

"Randy," said Slocum, "I know there were more of them in the house when they started shooting, but I'm damned if I can see any sign back here of where they might have gone."

"Well, they couldn't have made it to the corral," said Randy. "We could see that from out front."

"That means that they're on foot," Slocum said. "They

had to make it into these woods back here."

"We could surround the woods," Randy said.

"We'd be spread out pretty thin," said Charlie Hope, who had just walked out the back door and had been listening to the conversation.

"Yeah," said Slocum.

"So what do we do?" Randy said. "Just let them get away?"

"Not hardly," Slocum said. "Let's all go back to the horses. Load up that boy that got killed. Then about half of you mount up and head on back to the ranch. The rest of us'll hide our horses out there and stick around. If anyone's watching, they might think that we all left."

"You think they'll come back to the house?"

"I think they'll come back for their horses meaning to light out," Slocum said.

They all moved back to their original locations in front of the house. A couple of the hands picked up the body of their fallen comrade and loaded it onto his horse. As they made ready to leave, Slocum and some of the others moved their horses in behind the trees. In a few minutes, the rest mounted up and headed out. Randy, Slocum, and some more of the Tipton men were hiding in the trees.

"How long are we going to wait here?" Randy said.

"Just as long as it takes," Slocum said.

"You pretty sure they'll show up?"

"What would you do if you were on foot out there?"

"I guess I'd come sneaking back for my horse."

"Exactly."

Out in the woods behind the house, Oscar and Brace sat down on the ground to lean back against tree trunks. Oscar was sniffling. "Brace," he said. "What're we going to do?"

"I ain't sure," Brace said. "I got to think about it."

"Maw's dead," said Oscar. "Maw and Hiram and Henley. Hell, Brace, our family's been cut to pieces."

"You think I don't know that? I know that. Hump and them's out somewhere around. We need to find them and join up with them. We can't fight them bastards just the two of us."

"We need horses."

"That bunch won't hang around our house forever," Brace said. "They'll get tired and go on home. Then we can sneak back down there and get our horses."

"And then go looking for Hump and them? How will we know where to look?"

"Maw sent them out to see what meanness they could do to Tipton," Brace said. "They'd ought to be somewhere between here and Tipton's spread. We'll find them all right."

They sat still and silent for a while longer, the only sounds were Oscar's sniffling and the chattering of birds and squirrels. A light breeze was blowing that occasionally rustled the leaves overhead. At last, Brace stood up.

"Let's ease ourselves on back down to the house," he said. "I reckon we've waited long enough."

Hump and the rest of the Beamer gang were on Tipton's ranch. They weren't far from the spot where they had killed Ace and rustled the cattle a few days before. The fence had been repaired, and they had cut it again. They had been looking for another batch of cows with another couple of cowhands watching over it, but they had not had much luck.

"Maybe we ought to ride on in closer to the ranch house, Hump?" Jefferson Davis Beamer said.

"It's too dangerous," said Hump. "Hell, they got a whole army of hands and that damned gunfighter in close to the ranch house watching for trouble."

"We sure ain't having no luck out there."

"Maw ain't going to like it if we don't do something," said Butcher.

"Shit, I know that," Hump said. "But I ain't intending to go commit suicide just to make Maw happy."

"Well, what'll we do?"

Hump sucked a finger of his right hand and then held it up. "There ain't much breeze," he said, "but there's a little."

"So what?" Butcher said.

"So if we set this grass on fire in about a half a dozed places, we can at least cause ole Tipton some damned headaches."

Butcher grinned. "You're right," he said. "Let's do it."

"Let's spread ourselves out real wide," Hump said. "Everyone got some matches?"

"Yeah," they all said.

"When we get well spread out, I'll wave my hat," said Hump. "Then all of us get down at once and light the grass on fire. You get your fire going, mount up again and head for that hole in the fence."

The five riders moved apart staying in line. They all dismounted and looked toward Hump. Checking the line and the distance between the men, Hump, still sitting in his saddle, took off his hat and waved it in the air. Then he dismounted, knelt, took a match out of his pocket, and carefully set fire to the grass. The others were doing the same thing. In another moment, they were all mounted up again and riding for the place they had cut the fence. When they had all arrived together, Hump stopped riding and turned in the saddle to look back at the result of their deviltry. The flames were growing. He grinned.

"That'll raise some hell with them," he said.

"It might even reach the ranch house," said Butcher.

"Good for them," Hump said. "Let's get on back to the house and tell Maw and the others what we done out here."

"Maw'll be just tickled," Butcher said.

Hump led the way, and they started riding. They had gone some distance before Hump slowed them down. He didn't want to run their horses into the ground. He stopped and reached in his pocket for the makings.

"Hey, Hump," said Butcher.

"What?" said Hump. "What is it?"

"Has the wind shifted?"

Butcher was sticking his wetted finger in the air. Hump sucked his own finger and stuck it up again.

"Damn," he said. "It has."

He turned around in the saddle to look back behind

them. Smoke was billowing on the range. He squinted his eyes and watched for a moment, and the black smoke seemed to be coming closer to them. He kicked his horse in the sides and started to ride fast toward home.

"Come on, boys," he said. "That's headed straight for our house."

13

Brace and Oscar eased themselves out of the edge of the woods just behind the house and peered around. The saw no sign of life. "I reckon they're gone all right," Oscar said.

"Hold on just a minute," said Brace. "We got to be sure."

"Well, I can't see no one. How're we going to be sure?"

"Well, now, you could just stroll on over there to the corral and start saddling up your horse and see if anyone shoots you. How'd that be?"

"It might be better than just standing here all damn day," Oscar said. He was tired of being treated like a baby brother.

"Wait a minute," said Brace. "Let's just ease on up to the back of the house. If there's still anyone out there, they won't see us."

The two Beamers sneaked out of the woods and crept to the back of the house. Both of them avoided looking in the direction of their dead mother. Their two brothers were in the house, so that wasn't a problem.

"What now?" said Oscar, pressed against the back wall.

Hidden in the clump of trees out front, Slocum noticed the dark wall of smoke building up in the sky. "Randy," he said, "it looks like Tipton's range is on fire back there."

"Yeah," said Randy. "It looks like it's pretty damn

close to the Beamers' place. I think we ought to get out of here."

"Let's hold off a little," said Slocum.

"Whatever you say, but a fire like that can spread awful fast. I seen them before."

"I know, but we've got a little time. If there's Beamers out there behind the house, they've got less. That fire will drive them out in a hurry."

"Yeah," said Randy.

Behind the house, Oscar was getting more nervous. "Brace, that fire's getting closer. We got to do something fast."

"There ain't no place we can run to," said Brace. "The only chance we got is to go for the corral."

"Maybe there ain't no one out there."

"Maybe. Hell, let's go for it."

"All right. Hell, they can only kill us once."

"Come on," said Brace, and crouching low, he ran for the corral. Oscar ran right behind him.

Slocum was watching the smoke. When he noticed the Beamers making for the corral, they were already almost there. Once they got to the corral, they would have a little cover before they had to come out again. He jerked up his rifle and fired off a shot, too quick. His shot nicked at Oscar's shirttail. The Beamers made it to the corral. Oscar went for a saddle.

"There ain't no time for that," Brace said. "Just grab a hackamore."

"Ride bareback?" said Oscar.

"We got to get going, boy," said Brace. He just about had the hackamore snugged down on his horse. Oscar grabbed another one and started fumbling with it. "Here," said Brace. "Give me that. You take this other horse."

While Brace put the hackamore on the second horse, Oscar swung up onto the back of the first one. "Where we going?" he said.

"Head out toward the road," said Brace. "We got to get out of the path of that damn fire."

Oscar rode to the gate and reached down to drop the pole which served as a gate. Then he kicked the horse in the sides and rode hard toward the front of the house. Three shots from the Tipton bunch dropped him from the horse's back. The horse ran wild, followed by several others that had been in the corral. Brace threw himself onto his horse's back and dropped to one side, riding with the spooked horses. He managed to get himself into the middle of the small herd, and they rode fast by the clump of trees where Slocum and the others were hidden. Slocum caught a glimpse of a boot over the horse's back.

"One's getting away," he said.

"Let's get after him," said Randy.

Slocum looked after the running horses. "We can't catch him," he said. "Check that other one over there."

Randy sent a couple of cowhands to check the body of Oscar. They came back and reported that he was dead as hell.

"Well," said Randy, "we better get moving before that fire gets any closer."

"Yeah," Slocum said. "Let's head back for the ranch."

They mounted up and turned their horses toward the road.

Hump and the rest of the gang rode hard ahead of the now-raging wildfire.

"It's gaining on us," Goofball McGinnis shouted.

"Shut up and ride," said Hump. "We'll make it to the house."

Just then Goofball's horse stumbled, throwing Goofball off over its head. He landed with a hard thump and rolled over three or four times. The wind was knocked out of his lungs. He tried to call out for help, but he couldn't make any noise. He lay on his back gulping for air. No one had noticed his fall. The horse managed to get to its feet and run after the others. Goofball watched it go, still trying to suck wind. At last he caught some breath.

"Come back!" he yelled.

No one heard him, or if anyone did, no one paid any attention. They seemed to ride harder and faster away from him. Panic-stricken, he got to his feet. He watched them for a moment. Then he yelled again. "Hey. Come back." He turned to look over his shoulder at the flames which were coming at him, moving faster and faster it seemed to the sorry wretch. He started to run. He ran ahead stumbling as he did. He knew that it slowed him down to turn his head and look over his shoulder, but he could not help himself. He frequently looked anyway, and each time he looked, he felt more helpless. He had a long run to escape the flames. He could not make it, but he could not just give himself up to a blazing death.

He stepped on a rock and turned his ankle, and it threw him to one side, and he fell hard on the rocky ground. "Ah," he cried out. "Oh God." He was out of breath again. He turned to look at the fire. Now it looked to him as if there was nothing behind him at all other than the roaring wall of flames with its billowing black cloud of smoke above. He could feel the heat. He knew that he was going to die.

"Goddamn Hump Beamer," he cried out. "Goddamn him to hell."

Hump and the others reached the house from the back. Some had started to dismount, but Hump suddenly cautioned them. "Something's wrong here," he said. "Get your guns ready and get down slow. Look around." They all dismounted with their six-guns in their hands. Hump moved toward the house. The others went in other directions.

"Hump," Butcher yelled. "The horses is gone. All of them."

Hump had stopped still already. He was looking at the back door standing wide open. Maw never left the door like that, he thought. He moved in closer, staring at the open door. When he reached it, he stepped inside. There were the bodies of his two brothers, Hiram and Henley. He stopped still for a moment. Butcher came running up to the back door.

"Did you hear me?" he said. "The horses is gone."

"I heard you," Hump said.

Just then, Butcher saw the bodies. "Oh shit," he said. "Where's Maw?"

"I don't know," said Hump. "I ain't seen her."

Skinny Clark stepped into the front door, which, like the back, was standing wide open. "Hump," he said, "your Maw is outside." He pointed to his right through the wall. "Out yonder by the back corner."

Butcher hurried out the back door and ran to the corner of the house. Hump followed more slowly. The two brothers stood there looking down at their Maw. In another minute, Jefferson Davis walked up.

"Maw?" he said.

"She ain't going to answer you, Jeff," said Hump. "She's gone."

"Maw and Hiram and Henley?" said Jefferson Davis.

"Yeah," said Hump. "And don't forget Billy and Ike and Harman."

"Say," said Skinny, "I don't see Goofball."

"We lost him back at the fire," Hump said.

"What?" said Skinny. "What do you mean we lost him?"

"Just what I said. His horse threw him. He fell. He's still back there."

"Well, we got to go get him," Skinny said.

"Hell, he's cooked already," said Hump. "Let's get mounted and get out of here."

"What're we going to do about Maw and the boys?" Jefferson Davis said.

"Leave them here," said Hump. "They'll be cremated."

"We can't do that."

"If we don't, we'll likely be cremated ourselves. If you want to take a chance like that, go on ahead and stay behind and dig some graves. Me? I'm getting out of here."

Hump walked back to his waiting horse, and the others watched him go. They looked at one another. Skinny looked at Butcher and at Jefferson Davis. Then he turned and walked after Hump. Hump turned in the saddle to look at his two brothers. "Well," he said, "you coming?" They ran after him and mounted up. The three Beamers and Skinny rode off toward the road. Hump turned toward town, and the others followed him. They had gone a ways before Butcher spoke up.

"Hey, Hump," he said, "where the hell're you headed?"

"I figure that fire'll take out our house," said Hump. "Then it'll come on out here to the road. It'll stop there. We'll get away from it all right if we're in closer to town. We'll move off the road in another mile or so."

"All right," said Butcher. He rode along with the others for a space in silence. Then he said, "Hump, what do you mean to do next?"

"What do you want to do, Butcher?" Hump said.

"Kill Slocum," said Butcher.

"Me, too," said Hump, "and Tipton. At least them two."

"All right."

Hump turned his horse off the road to the right. The others followed him.

"I'd like to fuck that little gal of his," Jefferson Davis said.

"We kill Slocum and Tipton," said Hump, "you just might get to do that."

"What about the rest of us?" said Butcher.

"All of us," Hump said.

"We can fuck her to death," said Jefferson Davis.

"That's the general idea," said Hump.

They all laughed at the thought. They rode on a little farther until they came to a side trail. Hump led the way onto it, turning in the direction that led away from the main road.

"Where's this go?" asked Jefferson Davis.

"You'll know soon enough," Hump said.

They moved along for a while in silence. Then they topped a rise, and Hump stopped his horse. The others rode up beside him. About a half a mile ahead and on the left side of the trail was a small log cabin nestled back in the trees. Smoke rose gently from its chimney.

"That there is old Yancey Jones's place," said Hump.

"I never knowed that was here," said Butcher.

"You never did get around enough," Hump said. "Now let me tell you about old Yancey. He's a goddamned hermit. No one comes to see him, and he don't go nowhere."

"How's he live?" asked Jefferson Davis.

"He keeps a little pissy-assed garden, and he raises goats. That's what he lives on."

"Goat meat and radishes?" said Butcher.

"Yeah. And whatever else is in his garden and goat's milk."

"I couldn't live like that," said Skinny.

"Well, we're going to," said Hump. "For a little while."

"What are you talking about?"

"We're going to hole up right down there," Hump said. "Won't no one come looking for us there. We'll wait a few days. Everyone will figure that we hightailed it out of here. They'll relax. Then we'll come sneaking out, and we'll kill them."

"That's good thinking," said Butcher.

"Let's go on down," Hump said.

They rode slowly down to the little cabin. When they reached it, they moved their horses into the yard right in front of the cabin. In a couple of minutes, the front door of the cabin was opened from the inside, and a couple of eyes peered out from the darkness.

"Who are you?" came a voice.

"Just some weary travelers," said Hump.

"What are you doing here?"

"Looking for a little kind hospitality."

"There ain't nothing here for you."

"We don't want much," Hump said. "Just a little bit to eat is all. We been traveling a long road."

"I think you're lying to me," said old Yancey. "I think your name is Beamer. I seen you around. You just live a few miles from here. You all get on out of here now."

"Hell, Hump," said Butcher, "you said the old son of a bitch didn't never get out."

The long barrel of an ancient Kentucky rifle poked out through the crack of the door, and Hump stiffened in the saddle.

"I'm telling you to ride on," Yancey said. "You ain't welcome here."

"That's mighty damned unfriendly," Butcher said.

"Naw, hell, that's all right," said Hump. "If he don't want us around, we'll just move on. Let's go, boys."

"What?" said Butcher.

"You heard me," said Hump. "Let's go."

He turned his horse and rode back out onto the trail, and the others followed him. Hump continued to ride away from Yancey's cabin. He rode until they were out of sight of the old man, and then he stopped.

"What are you up to?" Butcher asked.

"I didn't want to take no chances on getting one of us shot with that damned old gun of his," Hump said. "We'll just wait a while. Then I want you to sneak back down there. Keep hid. Take your rifle with you, and wait for that old fool to show hisself. Then drop him. When we hear your shot, we'll come a running to join you."

"What if he don't come out?"

"He'll come out. He's got to take care of his critters, don't he? Now get going on down there."

Butcher dismounted, took his rifle, looked back at Hump, then started down the edge of the trail toward Yancey Jones's lone cabin. Soon he found a spot beside the trail where he had good cover and a clear view of the cabin. He settled in to watch and wait.

14

Brace Beamer wandered the prairies and the woods alone wondering just what the hell he was going to do with himself. He was all alone, and he was wanted by the law. Well, the law was no problem, but there were those damned dodgers that someone had put out offering a reward for him and for Hump. He wondered where Hump might be just now. Hump had gone out to cause mischief on the Tipton spread, and he had not been seen again, at least not by Brace. Brace had never been alone before, not really. He had gone to town a few times by himself, but he always knew that Maw and his brothers were there at the ranch. Now Maw was gone, and so were several of his brothers. As far as he knew, Hump was still alive and so were Butcher and Jefferson Davis. But where in hell were they?

He was getting hungry and thirsty. He knew where there was a stream not far away, so he decided to ride over there and at least quench his thirst. It ran across the Tipton place, but he did not want to go that way. That was where the fire had started, and for all he knew, it was still raging. The looked in that direction, and he could still see the black smoke rising. The stream ran across the road and into the woods on the other side. He could find it over there. He just had to be careful when he crossed over the road. He did not want to be seen by anyone. He was fair game now with those damn dodgers out.

He felt in his pockets, but he knew before he did so

that there was nothing in them: no money, no chaw, no makings for a smoke. His ass and his legs hurt from riding bareback so long. He knew that he had to think of something. He had to do something to change his luck. He couldn't just go on like this. If only he could figure out where to look for Hump and the others. He stopped at the edge of the road to listen for any riders that might be coming along. Hearing no one, he crossed hurriedly, and in a few more minutes, he had found his way to the stream on that side of the road. He dismounted by sliding off of the bareback horse, and he staggered down to the water's edge. Dropping to his knees and then lowering himself to his belly, he dipped his face in the cool, fresh water and drank his fill. At last he rolled over onto his back to rest.

He was still hungry, but he felt a little better after the long, cool drink. He was sore from the long ride with no saddle. He wondered where he could find one. Of course, he would have to steal it. He had no money. He tried to think of places where he might locate a saddle to steal. The Tipton place was the nearest, but that would not be a good place to ride into alone. Tipton had an army of cowhands and that damned gunslinger watching over the place. He hated to think about climbing back onto that damned horse without a saddle, but his hunger was getting ferocious. He had to find something to eat before long. He fancied that he might be dying of hunger. Of course, he was not.

Deciding that he could put it off no longer, Brace sat up. His eyes opened wide. He looked all around. There was no sign of the horse. Damn it. He had been so anxious to get himself a drink that he had not bothered tying the animal. The son of a bitch had wandered off. He stood up and walked over to where he had left it, and he looked around in all directions. He could not see the horse anywhere. He wondered where it could have gone. The woods were thick. It could have gone in any direction. It might have gone back out onto the road. Hell, it might even have headed back toward home. What would a horse do, he wondered, if it went back home and found the whole place burned to the ground?

Then he started to think about the home place. It might be possible that the fire had skipped over some stuff. There had been food in the house. And there were those loose horses that had run off when he and Oscar had made their run for it. Some of them might still be around. Maybe a saddle had survived the conflagration. Well, he decided, there was nothing to do but make the long walk back to the house, or to where the house had been. He started hoofing it.

Butcher had been waiting in his hiding place for so long that he had dropped off to sleep. He came awake with a start. Rubbing his eyes, he looked toward the cabin. It was as it had been. He squirmed around in an attempt to relieve some of his limbs which were beginning to ache from sitting so long in the same position. Then he saw the door open and old Yancey step out front. The old man looked up and down the road as if to assure himself that he was indeed alone. Butcher raised his rifle to his shoulder and took careful aim. He could only afford one shot. He squeezed the trigger, and the rifle bucked against his shoulder. The lead smashed into the old man's chest dropping him instantly. Butcher stood up. In spite of his weary limbs, he grinned a satisfied grin, and he started walking toward the cabin.

Brace made it back to where his home had been, but he found nothing but piles of ashes. There was no house, no corral, no horses. The bodies of his mother and of his two brothers were charred beyond recognition. The fire was out, but everything was still smoldering and smoking. Exhausted, he sat down on the blackened earth, but he yelped and jumped back up. The ground was hot. He slapped at his own ass, afraid that he had set his pants on fire. He looked around once more, wondering what he was going to do. It looked to Brace as if the fire had burned in a diagonal line from where it had started on the Tipton spread across the Beamer place to the road where it had stopped. That meant that not all of the Beamer place had burned. There was some wild country off to the northwest that had not been touched. But that would do him no good.

He thought about all the things that had been there that he was so desperate to have. There had been money. He knew that. Maw always kept some money around. There had been horses and saddles. And there had been food. Lots of food. He wanted all of those things. He decided to rummage through the burned mess that had been his house. Walking into the middle of the pile of burnt wood, he made his way to where the fireplace still stood, its rocks unharmed by the flames. The things that had been sitting on the mantel were burned. He tried to think where Maw had last put her money, but he could not remember where it had been. She had moved it occasionally by habit, so that her boys would not try to sneak any of it out.

He found a chunk of burned black beef, and he picked it up, but it was so hot that he dropped it again. He looked around until he found a kitchen knife. Its wooden handle had been burned away, and the blade had turned black, but it was still in good shape beyond that. He picked it up and dropped it, yelping and flapping his fingers. He took the rag out of his back pocket and carefully wrapped it around the knife where the wooden handle had been. Then he took the knife and stabbed it into the beef. Lifting the beef in this manner, Brace took a bite. It was burned black. Eating it was like trying to eat a piece of burnt wood. He forced himself to eat several bites before he threw it away. Then he stood there looking around, feeling helpless and alone. For a brief instant he thought about burying the remains of his mother and brothers, but he could not even bear to look at them. He decided that were just as well off left as they were.

Then he thought about the stolen Tipton cattle. Almost surely they had escaped the fire. They would have run into that wild part of the Beamer spread where the flames did not reach. They would still be there. Cattle. Lots of cattle. Steaks and briskets and ribs. He was so hungry that his belly was growling at him almost constantly, and the few bites of charred beef he had forced down had only served to make it worse. He would go out and slaughter a fresh beef.

He thought about the problems related to that task. He had no horse and no rope. It would be a long walk to the cattle, and that, of course, was if they were where he figured they would be. He had his six-gun and he had a knife. If he could last long enough, and if he could find them, he should be able to kill one and cut it up, or at least, cut some choice slices off of the carcass. Then he could—He stopped short. He had no matches. He thought about the fact that everything around him was burned, and he had no way of starting a fire. And he did not even like rare beef. But what choice did he have? He did not like being hungry. He did not intend to starve to death. He picked up the knife again, and he started walking toward the unburned portion of the Beamer spread.

The little cabin was crowded, but it was much better than wandering the countryside worrying about who might happen along. Hump, Butcher, Jefferson Davis, and Skinny Clark were sitting around on anything they could find to sit on, some of them had their feet propped up on the one small makeshift table. They were all eating goat meat and drinking either water or goat's milk. Butcher took a long swig of the milk and wiped his mouth with his sleeve.

"Damn, I wish we had some good whiskey," he said.

"I'd go for any old whiskey right now," said Skinny.

Jefferson Davis stood up and looked on one of the shelves on the wall. "Are you sure we looked everywhere?" he said. "I can't believe that old son of a bitch didn't drink no whiskey."

"He was a goat man," said Hump. "Hell. He didn't need nothing else."

"I don't know about holding up here for several days like you said without no whiskey," Butcher said.

"And what do we do whenever we finish off this damn goat's milk?" said Jefferson Davis. "Anyone here ever milked a damn goat?"

"We'll drink water," Hump said. "Stop your bellyaching. We're safe here at least."

"Safe and sorry," said Butcher.

"Well, you ain't nearly as sorry as old Yancey, now are you?" Hump said. "He worked all them years building this place and fixing it up to suit just his own personal comfort, and now he's dead and laying out there in the woods for wolves and such to eat, and we're in his house with a warm fire and food, and no one knows we're here."

"So how long do you think we need to stay here, Hump?" Skinny asked.

"I'd say a couple a days, maybe three. They'll have figured that we lit out by then."

"Then we lay beside the road to catch Slocum and Tipton?" said Jefferson Davis.

"We tried that before," Hump said. "No. I think we'll just ride right in and attack the ranch house."

"Hell," said Butcher, "we tried that before, too, and it didn't work none too well."

"They got a army in there just waiting for something like that," said Skinny. "And there's only just four of us left."

"We'll even things up a little," Hump said. "You know that hardware store in town?"

"Sure."

"Well, they sell dynamite in there."

"We can't go into town," said Jefferson Davis. "Someone'll spot us for sure and then the whole town'll be after us."

"We'll go in way late at night," said Hump. "When everyone's asleep and everything is closed and locked up. We'll bust in that place and steal some dynamite. A bunch of it. When we attack that ranch house, we'll light them sticks and throw them at the house and at any cowhands we see outside."

Jefferson Davis's eyes lit up. "Hey," he said, "that sounds like it just might work."

"Sounds like fun, too," said Butcher, who was well named.

"When we kill them bastards," said Hump, "we'll steal

all the money they got around the place, and then we'll
light out. We'll get ourselves on over to the nearest town,
and then we'll have us some good whiskey."

"And women," said Butcher.

"Lots of good whiskey and lots of good women,"
Hump said. "Now, you think you can wait here three days
for something like that?"

Brace thought that he would drop dead from exhaustion
and hunger several times as he walked the long walk toward the still-green part of his family's spread. His legs
were hurting him so bad that with each step he thought
that he would just quit right then and there and lie down
and die. He had been sore at first from the bareback riding, but now he had all that walking added to it. He had
never walked so much in his life. The muscles of his
calves and of his thighs ached, and his hip joints were in
terrible pain. He was gasping for breath, and on top of all
that, his hunger pangs were now excruciating. He walked
along with his eyes half shut and his jaw hanging,
breathing in and out through his open mouth.

Once he scared up a jackrabbit, and he jerked out his
revolver and wasted three shots before it disappeared
again into the thicket. He continued walking, but for
awhile he watched carefully in case he should flush something else out. He did not. He was on the verge of giving
up hope. He had not seen a sign of any cattle. He was far
away from any human, far away, that is, for a man on
foot. He was about to drop down to a sitting position and
just give it up when he felt something squishy underfoot.
He looked down. He stepped back.

"Cow shit," he said. "Fresh cow shit."

The cattle had to be somewhere near. He looked all
around. Over the next rise there was a little draw. There
was good grass down there. It would be a good place for
the cattle to gather. He hoped that the dumb, stupid beasts
were smart enough to find it, and he hoped that he had
enough strength left in him to get over there. The thought
gave him some renewed strength and determination. He
walked faster for awhile, but then he was forced to slow

down again. The new hope had not given him that much new energy. He kept walking though, moving up the rise, heading for the draw on the other side. He stumbled, and when he fell he cracked a lip on a rock. "Ow," he mumbled. He reached to feel the lip and brought away a hand with blood on it. "Damn," he said. He tried to get up, but he lacked the strength.

He rolled over on his back looking up at the sky, and he saw some buzzards circling high overhead. "You watching me?" he yelled, but his yell was not very loud. "You nasty shits waiting for me to die?" He tried to sit up, but he could not. He lay there staring at the circling buzzards, imagining that they were watching him, waiting for him to lie still so they could come down and pluck out his eyes. That would be the first thing they would go for, he figured, the eyes. His thoughts drifted back to his warm home with Maw laying out a fine meal on the table. He thought of the bread she made, and the gravy and the meat she cooked, mostly stolen beef and always well cooked. He thought about the meals at home with his Maw and his brothers, and then he wondered where his surviving brothers could be. He wondered if he had any surviving brothers. And then he drifted off to sleep.

He woke up when he felt a heavy weight on his chest and stomach. He woke up slowly, and he had trouble opening his eyes. Then he saw the buzzard sitting on his chest. He had never seen one that close. He screamed and slapped at it. Slowly the surprised bird lifted itself with its broad wings, and then he saw that there were two others that had come down with it. They, too, were rising up in the air. He pulled out his six-gun and fired three wild shots at them. Then the gun was empty. He had not reloaded back there when he shot at the rabbit. He sat up shivering from the horror of what had almost happened to him. He reloaded the revolver, but it took him a long time because he was weak and he was shaking so. At last he made a supreme effort and struggled to his feet. He started moving again slowly up the rise.

15

"Slocum," said Tipton, "I wish you'd take me into town to see poor ole Seth. I'm wondering how he's coming along."

"I'd be glad to, Carl," Slocum said. "I think we ought to take along a couple of other boys with us."

"You think that's necessary? What Beamers are left have probably lit out for parts unknown."

"I hope you're wrong about that," Slocum said.

"You hope I'm wrong? What for?"

"If they've got out of here, I suspect that they'll be coming back one of these days. I'd just as soon we got rid of them all right away. Anyhow, Carl, I've seen their kind before. I don't think they'll give up so easily."

"Well, we can take Randy and one of the other boys. Randy can pick him."

Myrtle came out of the kitchen just then. "Did I hear you talking about going into town?" she said.

"That's right, Mama," said Tipton. "And don't look for us back tonight. It's likely going to be late, and I think we might just have to spend the night in town."

"All right," she said, "but try to remember to fetch me out that calico from Hefner's I ordered. It's bound to be in by now."

"I'll fetch it," Tipton said.

In a short while Tipton, Slocum, Randy Self, and Charlie Hope were riding into town. As they rode along, Charlie

Hope spoke to Randy. "Randy," he said, "I ain't complaining, but how come you and me gets to go into town? Do they think that them Beamers is still hanging around?"

"Slocum thinks they might be," Randy said. "I think the boss thinks that they lit out—what's left of them. But Slocum likes to be sure."

"I guess that's a good thing," said Charlie. "Say, did I hear right? Are we likely to stay the night in town?"

"That's what the boss said."

"Carl," said Slocum, "what are you really up to? It won't take so long to visit the sheriff and find out how he's doing?"

"Well, I got me some things I want to do," said Tipton. "We've had a bunch of trouble, and I feel the need to cut loose a bit. You know what I mean?"

Slocum thought about the saloon girl, Bonita, and he said, "Yeah. I think I know."

They did not talk much the rest of the way into town, and they had no surprise encounters with the Beamers or with anyone else. When they arrived in town, Tipton told Randy and Charlie to go on and have some fun. He and Slocum went into the rooming house where the sheriff was lodged. When they stepped in the door, Seth sat up and smiled.

"Carl," he said. "Slocum. It's good to see you."

"It's good to see you looking so good," said Tipton. "For a while there it looked like we was going to lose you."

"It'd take more than two bullets from that goddamned Hump Beamer to kill me," said Seth. "Say, have you got that son of a bitch yet?"

"Not yet," said Tipton. "Least, not that we know of."

"What do you mean?"

"We went over to the Beamers," Slocum said. "We tried to keep it legal. I asked the old woman to turn over Hump and Brace to us. She had two other boys in the house with her, but neither one of them. They started shooting at us, and we shot back. Killed all three of them. Then we saw a prairie fire coming at us from over on your range, and we lit out. It burned out a part of your range and a good part of the Beamer place, including the house. Someone might have been caught in the fire, but we don't know."

"I see," said Seth. "Carl, why don't you send some riders out to scout over that burned area? See what they can find."

"That's a good idea," Tipton said. "I'll take care of it first thing in the morning."

"It's a good thing ole Aubrey had them dodgers made," Seth said. "With me laid up like this and the marshal not due to come for a spell, I don't know what else we could've done about that bunch."

"That Beamer bunch is sure enough a bad one," Tipton said.

"It sure is."

"We'll get them all," said Slocum. "Don't worry none about that."

"Slocum," said the sheriff, "let me go on record right now. I don't care how you do it. Just get them."

Tipton wanted to go over to the Hogneck, so Slocum went along with him, even though he thought it was a little early. They had a couple of drinks, and Bonita appeared. Slocum figured that was it. He was right. Tipton went off with her in just a few minutes, leaving Slocum alone with a mostly full bottle of bourbon that was already paid for. Slocum finished the drink in his glass, got up, and carried the bottle to the bar.

"Goosey," he said, "you want to hold on to this bottle for either me or Mr. Tipton? Whichever one comes along first."

"Sure," Goosey said.

"Remember," Slocum said. "It's paid for, and I know how full it is."

"Why, Mr. Slocum," said Goosey, "do you think I'd try to put one over on you?"

"In a minute," Slocum said. He walked out of the Hogneck and across the street to Harmony's eating place. He found the place pretty busy, but he did find an empty table and sat down. Harmony made it over to him finally and asked what he wanted.

"Just coffee for now," he said. "I ain't in a big hurry, so take care of your other customers."

"Thanks," she said. She did bring him some coffee in just a few minutes. Slocum sat drinking the coffee for maybe a half hour before the customers started to clear out. He ordered a meal finally, and when Harmony brought it out, the place was empty except for Slocum.

"You want to join me?" he asked.

"I've got some cleaning up to do," she said. "You go on and eat, and I'll join you as soon as I can. All right?"

"Sounds fine."

Slocum tied into his meal, and it was a good one. He had just finished when Harmony brought him some more coffee. She also brought a cup for herself and sat down with him.

"That's better," he said.

"What's better?"

"Well, I've got a full belly, and now I've got good company."

She smiled and sipped some coffee. "You're not bad company, yourself," she said.

"You going to have much of a break here?" Slocum asked her.

"I won't have much business for a few hours," she said. "Come to think of it, it's hardly worth staying open."

She got up and went to the front door and locked it. Then she put a handwritten sign in the window that said when she would open again. She walked back to the table where Slocum was sitting. "I've got a more comfortable place in the back room," she said.

Slocum stood up. "Well," he said, "let's go."

They carried their cups with them to the back room where a large, stuffed couch was waiting, and they sat down side by side putting the cups on the table that stood in front of the couch. Harmony turned her face toward Slocum, and he leaned over to kiss her. It was a gentle kiss, but then she reached around him with both arms and kissed him hard. In another moment they were probing each other's mouths with their tongues. Slocum reached for a breast and squeezed it. Harmony moaned with pleasure.

Across the way in an upstairs room of the Hogneck, old Carl Tipton was yanking off the last piece of clothing from the body of Bonita. She was panting in anticipation. He tossed the item aside and crawled on top of her, leaning down to kiss her lips. He managed to get both his hands on her ample boobs, and he squeezed and kneaded and fondled them. Then he broke away from the kiss and scooted backward until he could kiss her breasts and suck her nipples. He lingered over them for a long time, and she squealed her delight. Then he scooted down even further, and when he started to lick there, she almost went wild. He stopped at last and crawled back up to kiss her on the lips.

"Oh, Carl," she said with delight in her voice, "you're just awful."

She wriggled around as he was trying to kiss her lips, and she wriggled until she was down between his legs. She took hold of his cock with one hand and squeezed his balls with the other. Then she slurped the cockhead into her greedy mouth.

It was late that night. Slocum was asleep in Harmony's back room. Tipton was sleeping heavily in Bonita's arms, and the two cowhands were snoring in one room together in the hotel. Outside Breakneck looked almost like a ghost town. Hump Beamer led his small and scruffy crew to the edge of town. They stopped and surveyed the town for a few minutes.

"Hell," said Butcher, "it looks to me like we could just ride in and take anything we want."

"Don't get careless," said Hump.

"All right," Butcher said. "So what do we do?"

"We'll ride around to the alley and go on into town that way," Hump said. "We'll go on down to the back door of the hardware store. But keep your eyes open."

They did what Hump said. At the back door to the

hardware store, they dismounted. Hump went to the door and tried it. It was locked, of course.

"Hand me that pry bar we brought along," he said to Jefferson Davis, and Jefferson Davis reached into his saddlebags and pulled out the bar, handing it to Hump. "Now, Jeff," Hump said, "I want you and Skinny to stay here in the alley and watch in both directions. If you see anyone, you let us know."

"All right, Hump," said Jefferson Davis.

Hump went to work immediately with the bar and broke off the lock. He stopped still for a moment after that, waiting to see if the noise had roused anyone. No one showed up.

"Come on, Butcher," he said, and the two of them went into the store. Hump went straight to the dynamite and grabbed up an entire case. He turned and handed it to Butcher. "Take this out," he said. He looked around some more while Butcher was taking the box outside. He found some matches, some boxes of bullets, and a couple of new rifles and six-guns. He took it all. He looked around, loath to leave everything else, but he knew that he had to stop somewhere. In this kind of work, time was the enemy. He hurried on out the back door, handing some of the stolen merchandise to each of the other three thieves. Then he mounted his horse.

"Hey," said Butcher, "what about some whiskey?"

Hump considered for a moment. "Why not?" he said, and they rode down a little ways to the back of the Hogneck. The place was closed up. Hump knew, though, that some people lived upstairs. No one stayed downstairs to watch the place though after it was closed. He did the same trick on the back door of the Hogneck as he had done on the hardware store, and again, he took Butcher inside. They packed out several bottles of whiskey, stuffed them into their saddlebags, mounted up, and headed out of town. They moved slowly and quietly until they had reached the edge of town. Then they rode hard for a couple of miles before Hump slowed them down again.

"Well, boys," he said, "what do you say to that?"

"I'd say that was pretty damn good," said Butcher.

"Yes, sir," said Jefferson Davis.

"A man couldn't hardly do no better," said Skinny.

"Say," said Butcher, "let's open up one of them bottles."

Hump pulled a bottle out and popped the cork. He took a long swig and handed the bottle to Butcher. Soon it had been passed all the way around and was back in Hump's hands. He corked it and put it away.

"Say," said Butcher, "what'd you do that for?"

"On account of I don't want no one getting drunk till we get back to the cabin," said Hump. "Hell, boys, we're toting explosives."

Brace was sitting on the ground leaning back against a tree. He felt satisfied. Not far away the partially slaughtered body of a calf lay. Flies buzzed over it. Crows had descended on it. Only the buzzards were driven away by Brace. He had developed a taste for raw beef. He decided that it wasn't nearly as bad as he had imagined it would be. And there was a fresh stream not far away, so he had plenty of water. But he had decided that he couldn't stay there forever eating raw meat and drinking water. A good meal would really hit the spot, and it had been a while since he'd had a glass of whiskey. He had managed to kill the calf without too much trouble, but he had not seen any of the horses. He really wanted to catch a horse so he wouldn't have to walk anymore, but he just had not had such luck. His feet still hurt and his whole body still ached, but he had rested up some. And the nights were cold with no shelter and no fire. He decided that he would walk out under the cover of darkness.

He stood up, took a deep breath, and started to walk. The straightest way back to the road would take him once again right by the charred ruins of his old home, but in the darkness he would hardly see it. He thought about the ghastly remains that were there, and he wondered if the carrion minded that they were so badly cooked. He wasn't halfway to the remains of the house when he started aching again pretty badly, but it was in the middle of the night and in the middle of nowhere. There was no way that he was going to stop. He recalled the buzzards that had come down to sit on him when he had fallen asleep. At night it would likely be wolves. He did not want that. He did not want to fight wolves in the dark. He kept walking.

When he reached his former house site, he paused for a while to rest. It was an uncomfortable and eerie feeling, sitting there so near the ashes of the house and of his mother and brothers. He could not really see any of it, but he knew it was there. He looked around in the darkness hoping to see a horse, but he did not. At last, he got up and started walking again. He made it to the road, and then he turned toward town. He was not sure why he had done that. He knew that he could not go into Breakneck. But he had no intention of doing that. He was just going in that direction. Hell, he thought, he couldn't walk that far if he wanted to.

He did not know how far he had walked, but he knew that he was walking alongside a part of the Tipton spread when he heard the sound of approaching horses. He ducked into the thicket along the side of the road. He was breathing heavily, and he was afraid that they people riding by might even be able to hear him. He wished that it was only one rider, so that he might have a chance to kill the man and steal his horse. They came closer. He could now see that there were four of them, all men. He heard them talking. They came closer, and his eyes opened wide. He was almost afraid to believe his eyes. He recognized his brother, Hump, and then Butcher, and Jefferson Davis and, ole Skinny. He sprang out from the brush, frightening the horses and shouting, "Hump. Butcher. Jeff. Skinny. God, I thought I'd never see you guys again."

16

Hump handed Brace the opened whiskey bottle, and Brace gratefully and greedily took a long drink. When he lowered the bottle, he felt woozy. "Goddamn," he said. "I sure needed that. Hey, have you guys seen the house since—"

"We seen it, Brace," said Hump.

"Hell," said Butcher. "I reckon it was us what set the damn fire."

"You set it?"

"We intended to burn off a bunch of Tipton's range," said Hump, "but the damn wind changed on us. What happened back at the house before that?"

"Slocum come with some men," Brace said. "They shot us all up. I'm the only one what got away from it. I was on foot all this time, and I been living on raw beef and water. That's all."

"Damn," said Butcher. "Didn't it make you sick?"

"It did at first, but I guess I got used to it all right. You can learn to eat raw meat if you have to."

"Hell, I didn't mean the meat," Butcher said. "I meant drinking water."

Everyone laughed.

"Well," said Brace, "someone give me a hand and let me climb up behind you."

"Jeff," said Hump, "take Brace up on the back of your horse."

Jefferson Davis reached a hand down, and Brace took

hold of it and swung up behind his younger brother. "Say," he said, "where the hell are we going?"

"We got us a new house, brother," said Hump, and he kicked his horse in the flanks and took off leading the pack.

"Slocum," said Randy Self, the next day back at the Tipton spread, "do you think we still need to keep all them guards out? Hell, there ain't nothing happened since we hit that Beamer house. We're getting behind in the ranch work here."

"Well," said Slocum, "I don't think the business with the Beamers is over with, Randy, but I suppose it would be all right if you wanted to cut the guards in half. I'd still send the boys out in twos, but maybe you could cut down on the fence riders, and maybe on the number of guards around the house."

"Okay," said Randy. "How long do you figure we have to keep our watch up like this?"

"I don't know. Till it's over with for good. I got a feeling, though, that it won't be all that much longer."

Randy headed off toward the corral, and Tipton came out of the house. Slocum turned to face him.

"Good morning, Slocum," the old man said.

"Morning, Carl," said Slocum. "You feeling all right?"

"Pretty damn good," Tipton said. "Myrtle says breakfast will be ready in a wink. You want to go on in and get a cup of coffee?"

Slocum took another pull on his cigar and threw the butt away off the porch. Then he followed Tipton inside. He knew why the old fart was feeling so good, knew what the devious bastard had been up to overnight in town, deceiving his good wife. Slocum did not like that about Tipton. Myrtle was a good woman, and she deserved better at the hands of her husband. When they walked in, Myrtle appeared bringing fresh poured cups of coffee. She had a bright smile on her face and greeted her husband and Slocum cheerfully. Slocum tried to be especially nice to her until he realized that what he was doing was probably pretty obvious, so he eased off it some. When the table was set and both Tipton ladies were seated, Slocum shifted his main attention to Jamie. That was easy enough to do, but soon that worried him, too. Jamie seemed to him to be acting much too familiar with him. She was saying things and giving him looks that he figured anyone could interpret as telling them all that she and Slocum shared some secrets with one another, and the secrets could be only of one kind. If she kept it up much longer, they damn sure would not be secrets any longer. He ate as fast as he could and took his refilled coffee cup out on the porch. In another moment, Jamie came out and joined him there.

"What's wrong with you?" she asked him.

"Ain't nothing wrong with me," Slocum said. "I just thought that you was coming dangerous close to exposing our little secret. That's all."

"Oh, you're just being a worrywart."

"You think so?"

"I do."

"You don't think that your ma or your pa noticed the kind of looks you was giving me? Or the tone of your voice? Some of the things you was saying?"

"I don't think they thought anything about it, one way or the other. Would you rather I turned on you again? The way I was when you first came out here?"

"Well, by God," he said, "it might be safer."

"I think you're just a nervous Nellie," she said. She finished the coffee in her cup and stood up. "I'm going to get some more coffee. Want some?"

"No," Slocum said. "I'm good."

Jamie went inside and Slocum set his cup down and left the porch walking toward the corral. He was really beginning to wish that this whole damn Beamer mess was over with and done.

Out at the old hermit's cabin, the Beamers laid out a spread. They had lots of goat meat, well cooked, bread, and whiskey. Brace ate until his brothers thought he would eat himself to death. "Anyone would think you been on a desert island by yourself for a whole fucking month," Butcher said.

"By God," said Brace, his mouth full of food, "that's just where I feel like I been."

"Hell, Butcher," Hump said, "leave him be. He'll need his strength tonight when we go out."

Brace looked up at Hump with curiosity in his eyes. He still kept chewing.

"I reckon you're right about that," Butcher said.

Brace's glance shot over to Butcher.

"What?" he said.

"What do you mean 'what'?" said Hump.

"You know what I mean. What you got planned for tonight?"

"Oh that," said Hump. "Hell, Butcher, go on ahead and tell him."

"I don't want to tell him, Hump," said Butcher. "I think that you had ought to tell him. It really ain't my place to do it. You're the oldest."

"Well, shit, I guess I can do it."

"I wish to God that someone would tell me something," said Brace.

"We're just going to take us a ride over to Tipton's place tonight," Hump said. "See if we can't kill us a Tipton and a Slocum."

"Maybe some others, too," said Butcher.

"Maybe steal a couple of Tipton women," said Jeff Davis.

Brace looked real solemn and sat quiet for a moment. "Have you thought this thing through real careful, Hump?" he asked.

"I've given it some thought," Hump said.

"On account a, you know, we tried it before. All we got was we got our family whittled down real good. There ain't that many of us anymore, and Tipton has still got that fucking gunman and his whole army of ranch hands."

"You're right about all a that, Brace," Hump said.

"Well then what—"

"Show him the stuff, Jeff," Hump said. Jefferson Davis reached into one of the saddlebags and pulled out sticks of dynamite, holding them out toward Brace and grinning.

"That shit'll narrow down the odds, don't you think?" Hump said.

Brace looked at them with wide eyes. "I reckon it just might," he said. "What's your plan?"

"We'll wait till late. We'll divide them blow sticks up even amongst us. We'll ride over to Tipton's and we'll cut the fence so his guards at the gate don't see us coming and give a warning. We'll each have a cigar, and we'll all light up. Then we'll ride in close enough to the house to toss these sticks with some degree of accuracy. We'll blow the damn house and anyone in it all to hell and gone."

Brace grinned wide at the thought, and then he took another big bite of the goat meat.

Slocum stayed up on guard that night. He and Charlie Hope were stationed at the house. In spite of his own cautions to Randy, things had been so quiet for a spell that he was beginning to relax. He was about to light a cigar when he thought that he heard a suspicious noise. He stood still and quiet. He had heard it. It was the soft sound of several riders approaching slowly, trying not to make too much noise. He wondered how they might have gotten past the guard at the gate, but he didn't really have time to consider that problem. He lifted his Winchester and chambered a bullet. Then he eased around the corner of the house.

"Charlie," he whispered. In another moment, Charlie Hope came hurrying over.

"What is it?"

"Listen."

They listened quietly as the riders drew closer.

"Half a dozen or so," Charlie said.

"Get over to the bunkhouse and get Randy up," said Slocum.

"Yes, sir." Charlie took off, keeping as quiet as he could and moving as fast as possible in dark shadows. Slocum leaned against the wall at a corner of the house and looked in the direction from which the sounds were coming. At last the riders came into view. He waited a little longer. Then he raised the rifle to his shoulder.

"Hold it right there," he called out. The riders stopped. Slocum noticed something peculiar. He could see small lights. One from each rider. They were all smoking.

"Now," someone called.

Slocum could not see well enough to tell what they were doing, but no shots sounded. Then he saw the first fuse catch and fizz and spew out sparks and then another and another and then one blew up a few feet away from him. The impact knocked him back and threw him flat on the ground. Other blasts sounded one right after the other. He had not heard anything quite like it since the war. It was deafening and it was frightening. One of the tosses carried to the front porch, and it took off a corner of the porch causing the roof to collapse in that same area. Slocum felt around for his Winchester. He had dropped it when the first blast had thrown him through the air. He couldn't find it. He pulled out his Colt.

Scurrying around in the darkness through the thick smoke and the dust and debris flying, he looked for a target. He could not find one. There were more explosions. He was afraid for the people inside the house. He hoped that they had the presence of mind to get out the back door. He heard some gunshots. The boys from the bunkhouse were coming. Then there was a blast over that way. One of the attackers had tossed a stick of dynamite at the ones coming from the bunkhouse. About that time, Slocum caught a glimpse of one of the mounted men through the hazy air, and he raised his Colt and fired. The rider had just lit a stick, and he jerked in the saddle, slumped and fell to the ground, the sizzling stick falling with him.

"Hey," Slocum heard someone cry out. "Get back."

A loud and lone explosion followed, and the attacking riders had ridden out beyond the range of their throwing arms in an attempt to escape the blast. Slocum looked around again, this time locating his fallen rifle. He ran over and picked it up. Raising it to his shoulder, he took quick aim and fired. He could tell that he knocked another one out of the saddle. Then they took off, tossing lit sticks of dynamite over their shoulders as they ran. The blasts were now nothing but an annoyance, for they too far away from the house to do any real damage, and they were getting farther and farther away all the time.

Randy Self came running up to Slocum's side. "Should we chase after them?" he asked.

"No," Slocum said. "We'd never catch them, and we can't track them in the dark. We'll try tracking come daylight."

"We had a man killed over there when they throwed that first dynamite at us," Randy said.

"Is that all?"

"I think so."

"I'd better check up on the Tiptons," Slocum said, but just as he turned to go around to the back of the house, they came walking toward him, all three of them. "I'm glad to see you're all right," he said.

"They didn't do no real damage to us, nor to the house," said Tipton. "Looks like they just blowed a corner off the porch is all."

"Sure tore up the yard," said Jamie.

"Killed one cowboy," Slocum said.

"Oh no," said Myrtle.

"Who was he?" Jamie asked.

Slocum looked over at Randy. "It was Tommy Gritts," Randy said. "He was killed by one of them blasts."

"That's a hell of a way to go," said Tipton. "We'd best take care of him."

"I've already got some of the boys doing that, Mr. Tipton," said Randy. Then he turned to Slocum. "This is all my fault," he said. "It was me asked you to cut down on the guard."

"I agreed with you," Slocum said. "It's no one's fault. If we'd had four here at the house instead of just the two of us, we wouldn't have heard them coming no sooner. I don't know how they got past our gate guards, but—"

"Someone's coming," Jamie said.

They all looked toward the main gate to see the two cowboys that had been stationed there running toward the house. "What happened?" one of them shouted.

"It's obvious they didn't come through the gate," Slocum said. "Likely they cut the fence somewhere along the way. No, Randy, it ain't your fault any more than it's mine or Carl's. But in view of what's happened here, go on ahead and put the guard back the way it was."

The Beamers rode hard for a couple of miles and then slowed down.

"Is anyone follering us?" Hump said.

"I don't see no one," said Butcher.

"They get Jeff?" Brace asked.

"Shot him off his saddle just as he lit a dynamite," said Hump. "I seen it clear. He fell with that lit dynamite and got hisself blowed all over the place."

"Damn," said Brace. "They got Skinny, too. There's just three of us left now."

"What're we going to do, Hump?" asked Butcher.

"We're going to kill us a Slocum and a Tipton," Hump said. "Ain't nothing changed."

17

Hump laid his plans carefully. He could not afford any more screw ups. He was down to two brothers. He did not want to lose another one. He found a hill beside the road that had a pretty good spot on top from which one could see the Tipton ranch house. It was much too far for a shot, but from there, one could see the comings and goings from the ranch. He figured out a schedule for himself and his two brothers so that all during the day, one of them was posted there.

"What do we watch for?" Brace asked.

"We watch for any time Slocum or old man Tipton goes out of there by hisself. If we see either one of them head for town without extra hands with them, the one who sees them get his ass back out here to the cabin. Then all three of us'll ride out to get him."

"What if it's Slocum and Tipton together?" Butcher asked.

"Same thing. If it's just the two of them, we'll go on out and take them."

They had watched like that for three days with no luck, but Hump had more patience than his brothers, and he kept them at it. One of the two men he wanted to kill, one or both, would ride out sooner or later, and he meant to be ready.

Slocum was sitting on the front porch of the Tipton ranch house smoking a cigar. He had a cup of coffee. Things

131

had been quiet around the ranch since the dynamite attack. Nothing had been seen of any of the surviving Beamers. The blasted corner of the porch had not yet been repaired because Tipton had not yet gone into town to order the lumber his boys would need to do the work. A long pole had been used to prop the sagging roof and keep it from falling in any further. The morning after the attack, Slocum had led a few men out on the road to try to track the Beamers, but their trail had disappeared after about a mile or so. He was wondering what he should do. They seemed to have disappeared. They could have fled the country, but he did not think so. He had known their kind before. Their mother and their brothers had been killed. They would be thirsting bad for revenge. They knew that they were outclassed as gunfighters by Slocum, but that would not make any difference. They would try to set up an ambush or something. They might even be out somewhere trying to recruit some help. He certainly did not believe it was over.

While he was mulling things over in his mind, the door opened and Myrtle and Jamie came out together. They were dressed to go riding. Slocum stood up and tipped his hat.

"You ladies planning to go somewhere?" he asked.

"We've got a bad case of cabin fever, I'm afraid," Myrtle said. "We thought about going to town, but we don't really need anything from town."

"And besides, we know," said Jamie, "that you'd make us take along a small army, and we don't really want that. So we decided that we'd just take a good long ride right here on the ranch."

"Well," Slocum said, "that ought to be all right. I'll just go get you some horses saddled. Any preference?"

"We'll just walk over to the corral with you," Myrtle said.

They walked to the corral where the ladies picked out their mounts. Slocum saddled the two horses, and the ladies mounted up. Then Slocum picked his own saddle off the rail and headed for his Appaloosa. Jamie turned and looked at him.

"You don't need to do that," she said. "We'll be all right as long as we stay on the ranch."

"I'd just like to make sure," Slocum said.

"Well, you can just catch up with us then," said Jamie, and she kicked her horse in the sides and took off at a gallop. Myrtle looked back at Slocum, shrugged, and hurried after her daughter.

"Shit," Slocum grumbled, and he continued getting the Appaloosa ready.

On the hilltop overlooking the Tipton ranch, Butcher Beamer was watching as the two women rode away from the corral alone. He stood up, his eyes wide. He could hardly believe his good fortune. The Beamer women were riding out alone. He watched long enough to determine the direction of their ride. Then he mounted up and rode back to the cabin as fast as he could go. Vaulting out of the saddle, he ran inside. Hump stood up when he saw Butcher's excitement.

"It's them women," Butcher said, panting. "The two of them rode off together. Nary a man along. Just the women."

"You sure about that?" said Hump.

"I seen it, didn't I? I was watching. They rode off just the two of them."

"Where was they headed?"

"I guess they was just out for a ride," said Butcher. "They headed out onto the ranch. I couldn't see nothing they was headed for."

"Come on," Hump said.

When Slocum had saddled his stallion, he mounted up and rode after the Tipton ladies. They had a pretty good start on him, but he wasn't in a hurry. He knew he was on the right trail, and he would ride up on them soon enough. He moved along easily, actually enjoying the ride. He sure couldn't blame the ladies for wanting to get out like this.

• • •

Jamie and Myrtle had not ridden hard and fast for very long, just long enough to get beyond Slocum's range of vision. The ranch in this area was rolling hills and patches of woods. Jamie figured that it would take Slocum a little while and a little effort to find them, but he would find them all right. She knew that. It was just a kind of game she was playing with him. They rode around a clump of trees and down the slope on the other side. Myrtle rode over to a small outcropping of boulders and stopped her horse. She dismounted and sat down on a rock. Jamie joined her there.

"You want to wait right here for Slocum?" she asked.

"We could," said Myrtle. "We don't want to give him too hard a time, do we?"

"Oh, I guess not. He'll have to look around some already to find us. This is a nice spot here anyway. This would be a nice place to build a house."

"Yes. It would."

"Maybe if I ever find myself a man I can stand, I'll put my house right over there."

Myrtle gave her daughter a look. "What about Slocum?" she asked.

The way she looked and the way she asked the question made Jamie wonder if her mother suspected what had been going on. "No," she said. "He'll never settle down. Not that one. He won't stay here. As soon as he knows the last Beamer is dead, he'll move along."

Myrtle cocked her head. "I think I hear him coming," she said.

"That's more than one horse, Mother," Jamie said.

"Maybe he brought some of the boys along."

Just then Hump, Butcher, and Brace Beamer came riding around the clump of trees. "See," said Butcher. "I told you. There they are."

"All by theirselfs, too," said Brace. "This is too good."

"Come on, Jamie," said Myrtle. Both women ran for their horses. Myrtle was in the saddle, and Jamie had a foot in a stirrup, when the Beamers descended on them. Myrtle was about to spur away, but she saw that Butcher had caught up with Jamie before she had gotten into the saddle. He was still mounted. He had reached out and grabbed her by the hair.

"Let go, you son of a bitch," Jamie said.

Myrtle tried to go to her rescue, but Brace and Hump rode up one on each side. Hump grabbed the horse by the bit, and Brace reached for Myrtle. She fought with him, but he dragged her from the saddle. In the meantime, Butcher had fallen from his saddle in his struggle with Jamie. He bore her to the ground with him, and they rolled over and over. At last, Brace wound up on top. His weight holding her down, he pinned her arms with his hands. She continued to struggle, and he slapped her hard across the face.

"Leave her alone!" Myrtle shouted.

"You'd best worry about your own self, lady," said Hump. He dismounted and stepped behind Myrtle, holding her arms from behind. Butcher got down off his horse and walked up to her leering. Myrtle kicked out viciously, landing a boot in Butcher's crotch. Butcher screamed and doubled over.

"You bitch," said Hump, turning Myrtle around and slapping her face, knocking her to the ground. As soon as she landed, he was on top of her. She reached out with one hand and scratched his face. He shouted and got hold of her free hand, and in another moment had her pinned down the same as Brace had Jamie.

"Ooooh, goddamnit," moaned Butcher.

Brace leaned down and planted a sloppy wet kiss on Jamie's mouth. She struggled, trying to twist her mouth away from his, trying to escape his fetid breath. When at last he stopped and lifted his head, she spat in his face.

"Damn you," he said. He turned loose of her left arm to slap her hard three times with his right, but she took advantage of her freed left to reach up and grab a handful of hair, pulling him over on his side. His one leg was still across her body. She wriggled out from under it, got up, and started to run. Brace got to his feet and ran after her, tackling her from behind. She fell hard to the ground, and he was on her again. This time she was facedown and he was crawling on her back.

Then, Butcher, recovered somewhat from the hard kick to his balls, stood up and walked over to where his brother was holding Myrtle down. "You got her good?" he asked.

"She ain't going nowhere," said Hump.

Butcher knelt just above her head and looked at her face. "Kick my balls, will you?" he said. He reached out and took hold of her blouse, ripping it aside. Myrtle struggled as best she could, but Hump had her down. Butcher began tearing at the undergarment, and soon he had a breast exposed.

"You insects," Myrtle said. "I'll see you all dead."

"Hell, lady," said Hump. "When we're finished with you, we're going to kill you."

Butcher reached for the exposed breast and squeezed it hard. Just then Slocum rode around the trees. He saw at once what was happening. He jerked the Winchester out of the saddle boot, cranked a shell into the chamber, and lifted the weapon to his shoulder. He snapped off a quick round, and Butcher screamed and jerked, his shoulder shattered.

"It's Slocum," cried Hump. He got up quickly and ran for his horse. Brace left Jamie and did the same. Slocum fired a second shot that tore into Brace's left hip. Hump managed to help Brace onto his horse, and the wounded Butcher got himself into the saddle. Slocum cranked another shell into the chamber and started to shoot again, but the women were left alone now, and he had to see about them. The three Beamers rode quickly away as Slocum hurried to the women. Myrtle sat up and was trying to straighten her blouse. Jamie got up to her feet and started walking toward her mother. Slocum dismounted about halfway between the two. He turned first to Myrtle.

"Are you all right?" he asked her.

"I'm not hurt, Slocum, just damn mad."

Slocum turned to Jamie. "I'm okay," she said. "You got here just in time though. They meant to kill us, Slocum."

"After they'd finished with us, they said," Myrtle added.

"Go get them, Slocum," said Jamie. "Kill them. Kill them all."

Slocum looked after the Beamers. He wanted to go after them. He wanted to kill them, but he did not want to leave the two women alone, not after what they had gone through. He did not want them to have to ride back to the ranch house alone.

"I will," he said, "but not till you're safe back at the ranch house. I hurt two of them pretty bad."

"Not bad enough," Jamie said.

Slocum caught up the two horses, and rode with the women back to the house. They started telling Tipton what had happened, and before he could shout any orders, Slocum was already riding. He went back to the place where the Beamers had attacked the women, and he started to follow their trail. Besides the tracks left by their horses, there was a blood trail, quite a bit of blood. He thought that one or two of the Beamers might die from their wounds even before he caught up with them. He followed the trail out to the road and then turned on the road. They couldn't get too far too fast, not losing all that blood.

Hump led his two brothers back to the goat man's cabin. He got them inside, but then he did not know what to do. The wounds were too bad to just bandage. He had no idea how to take care of a shattered shoulder or to deal with a bullet in the hip. Brace's entire right leg was blood soaked, and Butcher had blood all over him from the shoulder wound. Both brothers were moaning and groaning. They had turned pale from loss of blood. Hump got them settled in the cabin, and then he paced the floor, trying to decide on a next move. His brothers were totally useless. They would die without medical attention. He knew that. And he also knew that he could not get it for them. They might as well already be dead. He thought about shooting them, but he could not quite bring himself to do it. If it was just one brother, he might have. But if he shot one of them, the other one would know it before he could do that one in. He did not want his brothers to know that it was he who was killing them. Better they die hating Slocum.

The other problem was that Slocum would be on their trail soon, and it would be an easy trail to follow. He did not want to be caught in the cabin by Slocum with only his two dying brothers by his side. At last he made his decision.

"You boys need a doc," he said. "I'm going after one for you."

"Well, hurry it up," said Butcher. "I'm bleeding to death here."

"Just hang on," said Hump. "Both of you. I'll be back before you know it."

He left the cabin, mounted his horse, and took off. He was not headed for town nor for the Tipton ranch. He was headed out. He was through. To hell with Slocum and to hell with Tipton. He was the only one left from his entire family, and he did not intend to see the family come to a dead end. From now on, he told himself, he would look out for Hump. The rest of them could all meet for a re-union in hell. He rode hard for the next county, and he wouldn't stop even there. Hell, he might ride all the way to California. Then he might get passage on a freighter and sail to China or some other damn place like that. He didn't want to see Slocum ever again.

Slocum followed the blood trail to the lone cabin in the woods, and he saw the two horses out in front. He stopped and waited, watching the cabin. He wondered where the third horse might be. He recalled all the ambushes the Beamers had set up. Watching all around, he moved in a little closer, and he saw that the two horses were bloody. They were the ones ridden by the two wounded men. The third man was still healthy, but the question was where had he gone? Had he just hidden his horse, and was he inside with the others? Had he gone for help? Had he abandoned his wounded brothers? Or was he hiding some-where along the trail? There were plenty of places to hide.

18

Slocum waited a while on the trail looking down at the cabin. He had no idea to whom the cabin belonged. He had never ridden down this trail before. But there was no doubt as to the ownership of the two horses out front. He wished that he knew about the third horse. Two horses out front most likely meant that there were two Beamers in the cabin, probably the two wounded ones, but he couldn't be sure about that. The third one could be hiding in there waiting for him. He could have hidden his own horse out back just to trick Slocum, make it look like he had gone off and left his brothers. Well, Slocum had to find out somehow.

He rode his Appaloosa a little closer, then off the trail. Tying the horse there beneath the trees, he moved through the tangle of woods until he was fairly close to the cabin. He noticed a foul odor in the air. He moved slowly toward the rear of the cabin, and the odor became almost overwhelming. He pulled the bandanna out of his back pocket and held it over his nose with his left hand, leaving his right free to go for the Colt if need be. Then he saw the body, decomposing, picked over by something, coyotes, crows, buzzards, something. He pulled himself away from it and moved up to the side wall of the cabin. There were no windows. He eased around to the front. There was no window there either, just the one door. Slocum moved stealthily across the front of the cabin to the door.

It was beginning to seem likely that there were only

the two wounded brothers inside. Slocum had seen no horse out back. There were some goats wandering loose around the place, but nothing else was there to be disturbed. Close by the door, he reached out and gave it a slight shove. It wasn't latched. It swung wide open, banging itself against the wall. There was no one hiding behind the door. Slocum eased out his Colt, cocked it, and stepped quickly inside. He saw the two wounded men. One was lying on a narrow bed, a cot really, the other was laid out on the table. He could not tell at first if they were alive or dead. Both men were bloody messes.

He stepped over to the nearest, the one lying out on the table. He was wounded in the shoulder and had lost a great deal of blood. From the shoulder down, he was covered in blood. Slocum reached out and took the man's revolver from his holster and tossed it across the room. Then he moved over to the one on the cot. His one leg was blood soaked. Slocum took his gun and tossed it. He was about to lean over to check on whether or not the man was alive, when the man's head rolled slightly toward him.

"Hump?" he said. "Is that you?"

Slocum looked the man in the face then, and he saw that it was Brace, the same one who had started this whole mess by trying to shoot Tipton in the Hogneck Saloon. His face was pale and gaunt. Slocum knew that he wouldn't last long. He turned his attention to the other one, the one spread across the table and covered with so much blood. He felt the neck for a pulse, but he couldn't find one. He put the side of his head down close to the man's mouth, and he could not detect any sign of breathing.

"Deader'n hell," he said.

"What?" said Brace in a feeble voice. "Hump? Did you bring the doc?"

"Can you hear me?" Slocum said.

"Huh?"

"Can you hear what I'm saying?"

"Yeah. I hear you."

"Well, I ain't your goddamned brother. It looks to me

like he ran out on you. Left you here to bleed to death. Your brother over yonder on the table is already dead."

"What? Hump run out on us? Who—Who are you?"

"I'm Slocum."

The name of Slocum seemed to put a little more life back into Brace. His right hand slapped for his gun, but he discovered that it was not there. Summoning all of his strength, he sat up and opened his eyes wide. He looked at Slocum with hate in his evil eyes.

"You son of a bitch," he said. "You've butchered my whole family."

"You brought it on yourselves," Slocum said.

"Goddamn you," said Brace, and sucking in a deep breath, he made a lunge for Slocum. Slocum stepped back, and Brace fell hard on the dirt floor, face first. Slocum stepped over and toed the body onto its back. Brace was dead.

Slocum wanted badly to ride out after the one remaining Beamer, but he thought about the poor wretch out back. Someone ought to notify—someone—about this situation out here. Besides that, if he just took off the Tiptons would not know where he had gone. He had to ride back to the Tipton Ranch and tell them the whole story. Then he could ride after the last Beamer. Holstering his Colt, he went back outside and studied the ground carefully. He determined that there had been three horses there, and that one had ridden off alone. It had ridden in the same direction it had been going when it came in. It continued away from the main road on the small trail. Slocum walked back to where he had left his Appaloosa. He mounted up and headed back for Tipton's place.

"I tracked them to a little log cabin on a trail on the other side of the road from here," Slocum said to Carl Tipton. "There was two horses there. I checked out back and found a body. It's in a sorry state. Been there for a while. Nothing else but goats. Inside the cabin I found two of the Beamers, both wounded. One was already dead. The other'n died while I was in there. He kept on calling for

Hump. The way I figure it, there's one of the bastards left alive, and it's got to be this Hump."

"Sounds like it to me," Tipton said.

"It appeared to me like the Beamers had moved into this cabin and killed its owner. I figure that was his body out back."

"Goats you said?"

"Yeah."

"Well, that has to be old Yancey Jones's place. I'll take some boys out there and clean up. I don't know what the hell to do with his damn goats. Maybe I'll take a ride into town first and talk with Seth."

"Wherever you go," Slocum said, "take plenty of the boys with you. I wouldn't want this to get right down to the last man and then lose you."

"Don't worry," said Tipton. "I'll travel with a small army everywhere I go. What're you going to be up to?"

"I'm going after that last Beamer," said Slocum. "He's already got too much of a start on me."

"You want to take a fresh horse? Maybe an extra riding horse or two?"

"No thanks, Carl. Me and my big horse will do just fine. I got to get going now. I'll see you back here as soon as I can."

"All right, Slocum, and you be careful, too."

Slocum mounted up and rode back to old Yancey's cabin. He gave it a quick check to make sure that Hump had not doubled back. Everything was just as he had left it. He climbed back into the saddle and started on Hump's trail. He rode the rest of that day, and then he had to stop for the night. Hump was making pretty good time, better than Slocum had expected.

Up early the next morning, Slocum started the day with only a slug of water out of his canteen. He poured some into the crown of his hat for the Appaloosa to drink. Then he saddled the big horse and mounted up. About noon, he came across a small and lonely cabin, the first since the cabin of old Yancey. He stopped, and a man came out the front door with a rifle in his hands.

"What do you want, mister?" the man said.

"I'm tracking a man," said Slocum. "Thought maybe he'd come by here."

"Who are you?" said the suspicious man.

"My name's Slocum. I work for Carl Tipton. The man I'm trailing is called Hump Beamer. He's a mean one. Killed old Yancey the hermit back down the trail. I've tracked him out this far."

The man lowered the rifle. "He come by here all right," he said. "I reckon I can trust you. He come in here a hollering, and I peeked out the door. He had his gun out and ready. I took my wife out the back door and we run and hid in the woods. When he finally left, he had took my best horse. Left me his old wore out one. He had et his fill of our food, too."

"So he got him a fresh horse," Slocum said. "Well, thanks, mister. I'd best be getting after him."

"Say, you'll need some food."

Slocum hesitated a moment.

"It's ready," the man said. "It won't hold you up much. Why don't you climb down and come inside."

Slocum's stomach was growling and complaining anyhow, so he took the man's offer. He climbed down and started to tie the Appaloosa. Then he looked up at the man. "You got a place I can water my horse?"

"Water and feed," said the man. "Follow me."

They went around behind the house where the man showed Slocum a stall with a trough of oats. There was also a watering trough nearby. "You can put him right in there," the man said.

"Thanks," said Slocum, turning the stallion loose. He followed the man into the house. A woman stood against the far wall looking nervous.

"It's all right, Nellie," the man said. "This here is Slocum. He's after that man that stole our horse. I told him he could have a bite to eat."

"Surely," said the woman.

Slocum stayed longer and ate more than he intended to, and when he had finished, the woman packed him some food for the trail. Slocum thanked them both kindly.

He went out back to get his horse and led it around the house. There near the front door he mounted up. The man was standing at the door.

"Slocum," he said, "if you do find that man—"

"I'll bring your horse back to you," Slocum said, "and don't worry. I will find him."

He tipped his hat and headed on down the trail. Now and then he slowed and checked the tracks. He was still following Hump Beamer. That was for sure. It was also clear that Beamer was still a good distance ahead of him. Slocum maintained a steady pace. He came to another home, and he stopped by to inquire about his prey. The people there said that a man had come by earlier, and he had obviously been in a big hurry. They had not even gotten a good look at him. It was unusual, they said, for the trail was out of the way, and there were not very many places along the way to stop. Travelers usually stopped. Slocum thanked them and continued along his way.

Hump Beamer did not know that Slocum was on his trail, but he strongly suspected that he might be. He rode hard with no regard for the horse he was riding. Hell, he had stolen the horse anyway. What did it matter? He knew that the animal was getting weary of the way it had been ridden, so the next place he came to, he stopped. He told the man there that he needed to trade him for a horse. The man refused, and Hump shot him to death. Then he swapped his saddle to another horse there. He went inside the house, where he was startled by a woman. He shot her, too. Then he rummaged through the house for anything that might be of some use to him. He found a few dollars which he pocketed, and he found some food he could carry along on the trail. He also found a couple of extra guns and some ammunition, and he found a spyglass. He took all that as well.

He was riding his fresh horse as hard as he had ridden the other two, but he stopped when he topped a fairly high rise. He turned around in the saddle to look back down the trail he had been riding. He turned the horse around and stared hard, squinting. Then he recalled the spyglass he had stolen. He took it out and tested it, finding just the right setting where he could see clearly way back down the road. There were places along the trail that were obscured by the curves, the rises and drops in elevation, and the trees that grew along the sides of the trail, but he had a clear view of the trail other than that for quite a ways back. He studied it carefully, starting with the closest part to him. He went back as far as he could. He saw no one coming along. He closed the glass up and put it away. He was about to turn his horse and ride on when something caught his eye. He squinted after it. It was a rider. He had just come into view from around a tree-shrouded corner in the trail.

Hump hurriedly pulled out the spyglass again and searched with it until he had found the rider. He focused as best he could. The first thing he noticed was the big Appaloosa horse. It was Slocum all right. The son of a bitch was still on his trail.

"Goddamn it," said Hump as he put the spyglass away for the second time. "Damn it to hell."

He turned the horse quickly, kicked and lashed at it viciously, and rode hard down the trail. He had to put more space between them. He had to get out of this country as fast as possible. He was riding his third horse, and that Slocum was still riding his own spotty-assed horse. It couldn't go on forever. It had to wear out sometime. He'd catch him another horse before too much longer. Then he was bound to be able to outdistance Slocum riding just his one damned horse. He was looking over his shoulder for any sign of Slocum, but, of course, there was none. He wouldn't even have known that Slocum was after him had it not been for the spyglass. He turned his head back around and saw a bridge coming up.

It was not much more than a footbridge, but it spanned a river too wide to leap, and its banks were too steep and the water too far down for a crossing. Just a few planks, barely wide enough to allow a wagon to cross over with basic rails on each side, the bridge was obviously pretty old. The horse's hoofs clattered against the boards as Hump raced across. Then an idea came to him. He stopped the horse quickly and turned around. He rode back to the bridge, stopped and dismounted. Reaching into his saddle bag, he pulled out the last stick of dynamite, left over from the batch he and his brothers had used to attack the Tipton place.

He crawled down under the bridge and tucked the dynamite into a nook there where it would stay. Then he fished around in his pocket for a match. Coming up with one, he struck it on the underside of the bridge. It flared up and then went out. "Damn it," he snarled. He felt for another match. Bringing it out of his pocket, he struck it and cupped the flame carefully in his hands. Slowly he moved it toward the dynamite, and he lit the fuse. It spewed sparks. Hump backed out from under the bridge as fast as he could and scrambled back up onto the trail. Hurrying back to his waiting horse, he climbed into the saddle and lashed at the poor animal. He rode away from the bridge quickly, stopped, and turned around to watch.

He was getting impatient, and then suddenly there was a roar and a flash. Flames shot up from the old bridge, and pieces of splintered wood filled the sky. A great dust cloud arose. The horse underneath Hump, neighed and whinnied and bucked. It threw Hump off, and he landed on his face on the dirt trail. The fall knocked all the wind from his lungs. The frightened horse ran off down the trail, leaving Hump there alone. Hump sucked hard for breath. At last, he was able to get back up on his feet. He looked after the horse, but it had already disappeared from his view. He walked down to where the bridge had been and studied the damage he had done. He was well satisfied with that, but now he was afoot. He considered his situation. He was still well ahead of Slocum, and the bridge being out would slow Slocum even more. Now all he had to do was find himself another horse, and quickly, too.

19

Slocum and his horse were both surprised and startled by the blast which came from somewhere up ahead. At first Slocum could not imagine who could be blasting up there. As far as he knew, the country was pretty desolate. Then, almost immediately, he recalled the dynamite attack on the Tipton place launched by Beamers. Maybe Hump still had some dynamite. But what the hell was he doing with it up there?

"It's all right, old boy," he said, patting the Appaloosa on the neck to calm it. "Come on now. Let's keep moving."

They rode on until they came to another small house beside the trail. Slocum stopped and called out. No one answered. He tried again. Still he received no response. He dismounted and went to knock on the door. Then he saw the body of the man lying close to the wall. He could see that the man had been shot. He stepped to the door to knock. When he hit it with his fist, it swung open. Slocum eased out his Colt and stepped inside. He saw a dead woman lying on the floor across the room. Damn, he thought. Hump Beamer has got to be stopped. He went back outside and dragged the body of the man into the house. Then he went out again, shutting the door tightly. He mounted up and rode on.

Hump Beamer was starting to limp. He thought that he had never walked so much in his whole life. He cursed the horse that had run off and left him. He cursed the settlers in the area for not having put their houses closer to the bridge he had blown up. Finally, he cursed Slocum for being on his trail. What did the son of a bitch care about anyhow? His whole family was dead, and he was on the run. Wasn't that enough for Slocum's damned revenge? What the hell kind of a man was he? He hobbled up to the top of the next rise in the trail, and then he saw the horse standing in the middle of the trail not too far ahead. He stopped and stared for a moment. It sure did look good there. It was just waiting. The dynamite blast had scared it, and it had run off. Now it was being a good horse and waiting for him to come on up. He smiled and walked on. When he got close, the horse bobbed its head and turned and walked on farther away. It stopped again.

"All right, horsey," said Hump. "Just stand still there."

He walked toward the horse, and it ran. Not far up ahead it stopped and stood still again, as if it were waiting for him again. Hump walked faster in spite of the pain in his feet.

"You stand still there, you son of a bitch," he shouted. As he approached it, it ran off again.

"Goddamn you," Hump shouted. He picked up a rock and threw it, and the horse ran even farther away. Now Hump ran after it, his feet tormenting him as he did. "Stop. Whoa. Wait up there, you fucking knothead."

The horse paid no attention to Hump's foul language or his threats. It trotted comfortably on ahead. Frustrated, Hump stopped running. He pulled out his revolver and fired. The horse jumped. It ran ahead fast this time. Hump fired two more shots, both of which went wide. As the horse disappeared around a bend in the trail, Hump dropped to his knees, worn out, and he started to cry. Between his whimpers and snivels, he cursed.

"Fucking knothead. Son of a bitch."

"That sounds like ole Yancey's place all right," said Seth, who was now sitting up in his bed, after listening to the tale Carl Tipton told him. "You say Slocum just went on after Hump?"

"That's right, Seth. I come into town with a half dozen boys to see you and tell you what the hell was going on. I figure we'll ride on out there and bury everyone, but I wanted you to know about it first."

"Well, I'm glad you came in to tell me," Seth said. "I'm still not worth a shit. Can't even get up and around without help. Tell you what. Let me swear you and your boys in as deputies. It's kind of late in the day though. You might want to spend the night here in town and ride on out to old Yancey's place first thing in the morning."

"Well, I reckon that does make sense," Tipton said. "Oh, yeah. Slocum says there's a bunch of goats out there. What do you reckon we ought to do about them?"

"I'll talk to Old Man Carter," said Seth. "He'll likely go out there and get them. Take them over to his place. He has some goats already, you know."

"Yeah," said Tipton.

"You don't need to bother with them."

"Okay," said Tipton. He rounded up the six cowhands who had ridden into town with him, and the sheriff swore them all in. Then Tipton said that Seth looked as how he needed some rest, and he and the new deputies left the room.

"Boys," he said, "I'll get us all some rooms for the night. We'll head out to Yancey's place with first light. In the meantime, how about some drinks on me over to the Hogneck?"

"Yes, sir."

Tipton led the way. They took up a couple of tables, and they all had a few rounds of drinks before Charlie Hope noticed Tipton getting the eye from Bonita who was up at the top of the stairs. Charlie looked away from his boss. Tipton downed his drink and stood up.

"Boys," he said, "excuse me for a while. I'll see you later. Maybe in the morning. I might just go on ahead and turn in."

Slocum stopped at the wrecked bridge. So that was what Hump had used the dynamite for. He not only slowed Slocum down, but he had inconvenienced everyone who used this trail. Slocum guessed that there wasn't a hell of a lot of traffic along the way, but even so, it was a crappy thing to do. He dismounted and walked to the edge of the bank. Looking down, he could see that there was no way to take his horse down that way. He looked upstream, but he could not see any difference. Looking downstream, it looked even worse. There was no way of knowing which way to ride to find a place where he could get down to the water to cross over to the other side. It was a toss-up. He climbed back into the saddle and turned right.

He had gone for an hour at least before he spotted the place. The banks were much lower and had a less steep grade. He could go down here. He turned his horse and moved down and into the water. The stream was fast moving, but it was not deep, so the crossing was not difficult. Soon they came out of the water on the other side, and Slocum rode back up the bank. Then he turned left to make his way back to the trail. When he reached the trail once again, he looked back at the wrecked bridge. He did not waste much time though. He turned his horse again toward Hump's trail. Hump, he figured, had already cost him at least two hours.

He had not ridden far when he noticed something peculiar in the tracks on the trail. He stopped to get a closer look. There were horse's tracks, of course, but now there were also the tracks of a man on foot. And they were not walking along together. Hump was on foot. Maybe he had spooked the horse with the dynamite. If so, that was real break for Slocum. It might help to make up for the lost two hours. Hump was not going to be moving fast afoot. Slocum moved ahead anxiously until the dark of night forced him to stop. He had not yet seen Hump.

Early the next day, Tipton gathered his new deputies together in front of the Hogneck. They mounted up and started to ride out to Yancey Jones's place. The ride took a couple of hours, and when they got there, it did not take them long to discover the three bodies. Tipton was tickled to see what was left of Brace and of Butcher there in the house, but the remains of poor old Yancey Jones almost

made him sick. The six deputies did not take it well either.
They all had to tie bandannas around their noses, and they
dug a grave right beside the body so they would not have
to handle it much. However, working that close to the
horrible carcass, they had to work in shifts. No one could
stand it for long. At last they decided the hole was deep
enough, and they shoved the body over into it and shoveled fast to get it covered up. All done, they gathered back
inside the house.

"Now what do we do with these here?" asked Hope.

"You know what I think?" said Tipton. "I think we
ought to burn them up, but a big fire might run off the
goats. I'd say dig a shallow grave across the road and
dump them in there."

"Just one grave?"

"That's good enough for them," Tipton said.

Hump had another horse. He had not stopped walking the
night before when Slocum had stopped to camp. He had
walked on until he saw some lights. He eased up on a
small house with a corral nearby. Luck was with him. He
had even spotted a saddle and tack on the fence rail of
the corral. Sneaking up, staying as quiet as he knew how,
he had managed to catch one of the horses and get it
saddled up and ready to go. He mounted it up and rode
it slowly over to the corral gate, really just a pole lying
across the gateway. He leaned over in the saddle, took the
post, and dropped it to the ground. Then he started to ride.
The other horses followed him out of the corral. Hump
laughed at that. The owner of those horses would spend
at least all day the next day chasing his horses. And he
would be cursing whoever it was who had done him this
dirty deed. The son of a bitch had ought to be giving
thanks instead, Hump thought. He was lucky. He could
have been killed.

Hump rode most of the night, and he thought that he
would just continue riding all day, but by noon, he caught
himself just before he would have fallen out of the saddle.
"Damn," he said, shaking his head and rubbing his eyes.
He couldn't afford to fall asleep like that. If he fell out

of the saddle and went to sleep right there in the middle
of the trail, Slocum would ride right up on him. But he
was falling asleep. He had to find a place to get some rest.
He watched carefully on both sides of the trail, and at last
he found a likely spot. He could move off of the trail and
hide his horse. He could find himself a comfortable place
up on the side of the hill there and get some sleep. Slocum
was still a good ways behind him, so he should have the
time. It wouldn't take too much, an hour or two, and he
would wake up and get back on the road.

Slocum came upon a man walking in the road with a rope
in his hands. He rode up beside the man.

"Howdy," he said.

The man looked up and grumbled something in reply.

"That your place I just passed back there?"

"It's mine."

"Well, what are you up to, if you don't mind me asking?"

"Some son of a bitch come along in the middle of the
night and turned out all my horses," the man said. "I
reckon he stole one and just let the rest go. A saddle was
gone, too."

"That'll be the man I'm after," Slocum said.

"You're after him?" said the man, stopping and looking up at Slocum. "Who the hell is it?"

"His name is Hump Beamer. He's a wanted killer, and
he's been stealing horses all along this trail. You can feel
lucky. He's killed some of the men whose horses he stole.
Killed a woman along the way, too."

"The dirty son of a bitch," said the man.

"Here," said Slocum. "Jump up behind me. We'll see
if we can't find you at least one of your horses. We're
going the same direction anyhow."

"Thanks, mister," the man said, and he climbed on the
Appaloosa behind the saddle. Slocum moved ahead. They
had ridden not much more than a mile down the trail when
Slocum saw two horses just up ahead.

"Look," he said. "Those yours?"

The man leaned to one side looking around Slocum

and saw the horses. "They're mine," he said.

Slocum eased the Appaloosa forward until he came alongside one of the horses. The man behind Slocum reached out real easy and dropped his rope over the horse's neck. The horse shook his head a little and nickered, but he gave the man no trouble.

"Can you take it from here?" Slocum asked.

"Yes, sir," the man said, "and I sure do appreciate your help."

He moved from the Appaloosa to the back of his own horse.

"No trouble at all," said Slocum. "I hope you get the rest as easy. I'll be getting along."

"I hope you catch that son of a bitch," the man yelled as Slocum rode ahead.

Hump woke up with a start. He had no idea how long he had slept. He thought about the spyglass that was gone with the damned horse that had run away from him. There was nothing to do but to get moving. First he stood up as tall as he could and looked over his back trail. He could see no pursuit. Good, he thought. He saddled the horse quickly, mounted up, and moved back out onto the trail. Then he started riding fast. He wondered where this damned trail would take him. It had to go somewhere, to some town or other, to another road, a real road, a main road that would take him to some city where he could maybe get lost in the crowds. He was still thinking about California and maybe a boat or a ship or whatever that would take him out to sea and to some exotic foreign country or to some islands somewhere out in the ocean. He might not have enough money for that. He might have to steal some somewhere along the way. At worst, he might have to agree to work for his passage. Hell, he reckoned that he could learn to be a sailor as well as any. The more he thought about it, the more he liked the idea, and he kicked his horse in the sides and lashed at it with the long ends of the reins to get as much speed out of it as possible.

• • •

Slocum felt good that the last victim of Hump had not been harmed and he had been able to at least help the man out a little bit. He did not think that he could be so far behind Hump anymore. Hump had stolen the horse sometime in the night, probably while Slocum had been sleeping. That meant that Hump had been awake into the night. Maybe all night long. Slocum had gotten a good night's sleep. That should give him the edge. And the farther along on the trail he went, the more he noticed that Hump was running his stolen horse. He was going to wear the poor thing out. Then he noticed that Hump had slowed down. He watched carefully, and he saw where Hump had turned off the trail.

It would be just like the cowardly bastard to lay up beside the trail in an ambush, so Slocum moved slowly. Then he saw the tracks return to the trail, so Hump had just pulled off for some reason and then moved back on. He followed the tracks, and he found where Hump had stopped to get some shut-eye. That's all it could have been. He found where the horse had waited, and he checked the droppings he found there. By God, he thought, I'm closing in on him. At last, I'm going to get the son of a bitch. He mounted his Appaloosa and moved back down onto the trail. As anxious as he was, he did not want to go rushing ahead. This was not the time to lose control. This was the time for extreme caution.

20

Slocum eased forward watching both sides of the trail. Obviously, Hump knew he was being followed. Otherwise there would have been no reason for him to blow up the bridge. He likely also figured that it was Slocum who was following him, and because of that he would do one of two things. He would try to move as fast as possible to get far away, and that plan, if that had been his plan, would have been practically ruined when he lost his horse for a while, or he would lay in ambush and try to shoot Slocum from hiding. That was the Beamer way. Slocum figured that Hump would be waiting somewhere along the way. Even if he was hurrying on, that was the safest way to figure it. Just in case.

Slocum wasted a good deal of time in moving off the trail and checking out possible ambush spots. He hoped that Hump was waiting for him. If Hump was rushing on, then Slocum was just giving him more time to put space between them. He couldn't take a chance though. With the way the trail was lined with trees and hills, he had to check out all the possibilities. So he moved slowly. He came to another house beside the trail, and sitting on the Appaloosa's back, he waited until a man appeared at the door. It looked safe enough, so he rode on in closer.

"I'm looking for a man who likely came riding by here," he said. "Not long ago."

"Only one rider's been by for two days," said the man.

"He passed by here about two hours ago. Riding like he'd kill his horse."

"That's my man," said Slocum. "Thanks."

He kept going. So he was about two hours behind Hump. He could catch him easily if it were not for the fact that he was taking so much time worrying about whether or not Hump was laid up beside the trail somewhere along the way. Two hours more. The thought made him more anxious, and he fought to keep his head. He continued to move cautiously and check out all possible ambush spots. He passed by another house, but there was no one home. Not much later, he came to yet another dwelling. The people there told him the same thing the last one had. A man in a big hurry had indeed passed by about two hours ago. The houses seemed to be getting closer together, and Slocum wondered if that meant that he coming close to some settlement or other. He was not familiar with this part of the country, so he did not really know what to expect up ahead. He kept going, still cautious.

Up ahead, Hump Beamer was riding hard. His latest stolen horse was breathing hard and sweating profusely. Hump saw a house beside the trail situated at the top of a rise that looked like it would have a clear view of the trail behind. He had passed by three houses. This one looked good to him though. He slowed the horse and rode up to the front door.

"Hey," he called out. "Anyone home?"

The door opened, and a man stepped out.

"What can I do for you, stranger?" the man said.

"I'm a weary traveler," said Hump. "I'm hoping you can spare a drink of water for me and my horse."

"There's a trough right over there," the man said, pointing to his right. "There's a gourd by the well, too. Help yourself."

"Thanks," said Hump. He rode his horse over to the trough and dismounted to walk the few steps to the well. He hauled up the bucket and dipped a drink with the gourd. The man of the house had followed him.

"That horse has been rode pretty hard," the man said.

"Yeah," said Hump. "I'm in a hurry."

He looked around and spotted a corral behind the house. It could not be seen from the trail. That would be a good place to hide his horse. Suddenly he had a couple of ideas. Either one would suit him. He could hide here and let Slocum ride on by. Then he could turn around and go back where he came from. With Slocum out of the way, he could kill old man Tipton for sure. Then he could hightail it out of there in just about any direction he might want to go. Or if it did not look like he had fooled Slocum, he could shoot him from inside the house. If Slocum figured out he was in there, he could use the man as a hostage, threaten to kill the innocent stranger. That ought to work on Slocum. He took his horse by the reins and started toward the corral.

"Say," the man said. "What are you doing?"

"Just putting my horse in your corral. You don't mind, do you? I think we both of us need a little rest."

"You said you was in a hurry."

"Well, I reckon I was, but it looks like my plans has just changed." He reached down and slipped the revolver from his holster and leveled it at the man. "Why don't you just put this horse away for me? You want to do that?"

"Sure," the man said. "You got no call to shoot me."

"Not as long as you do what I say," said Hump. "Here. Take the horse."

The man put the horse in the corral and shut the gate. Then he turned to Hump and waited. Hump gestured with his gun toward the front of the house.

"Let's go inside and relax a spell," he said.

"Mister?" said the man.

"Well, what is it?"

"My wife is in the house, and—"

"Well then, take me on in to meet her. Let's go."

The man led the way to the front door and opened it. He looked back over his shoulder at Hump.

"Go on," Hump said.

The man stepped inside and Hump followed right behind him, shutting the door. The wife was busy preparing a meal. She looked around and saw Hump and saw his gun.

"Oh," she said.

"Now don't be afeared, little lady," said Hump. "You and your hubby here is just going to give me a little hospitality is all. Looks to me like you're a fixing a meal up. That's good. I'm right hungry, and I ain't et a good home-cooked meal in a while. Really, not since my dear ole mama died."

The woman looked at her husband in desperation. "Lonnie?" she said.

"It's all right, Etta," said Lonnie. "Just do what he says. When he's fed and rested up he'll be on his way."

"Just keep on working on that meal," Hump said. "And you, Lonnie, you just put yourself over there by that window and keep watching the trail back the way I come from. You tell me if you see anyone coming this way."

Lonnie moved to the window to watch.

"Say, Lonnie," said Hump, "you got any guns in here?"

Lonnie hesitated. He decided though that he had better tell the truth. "I have a rifle," he said. "I use it mostly to hunt squirrels."

"Where is that squirrel gun?"

"It's over there in the corner," Lonnie said, nodding his head, "kind of behind that bureau."

"You just keep your eyes on the trail," said Hump. He moved to the corner and got the rifle, taking it with him to the bed. His six-gun still in his hand, he stretched out on the bed, his dirty boots messing the clean quilt. He propped the rifle against the headboard. "You got some coffee made, Etta?" he said. "Seems like I can smell coffee."

"Yes," she said.

"Fetch me a cup over here," Hump said. "By the way, you all can call me Hump. That's my name. At least, that's what everyone has called me all of my life. Since we're all friends here, we can call each other by our first names. Don't you think so?"

Etta handed a cup of coffee to Hump. "Yes," she said.
"I reckon so."

"You see anything out there, Lonnie?"

"No sir," Lonnie said.

"Well, just keep a watching."

Hump slurped from the coffee cup. "Ow," he said.
"That's hot."

"I'm sorry," Etta said. "It was just made fresh."

"Damn."

"I'm really sorry."

"Oh, hell, Etta, that's all right. It ain't the first time
I've blistered my tongue on hot coffee. You just keep
busy with that there meal, and Lonnie, you keep on a
watching the trail. I don't want to see your head turn
around this way no more."

"Yes, sir."

It wasn't much longer before Etta had the meal prepared. She set the table with three places and put the food
on. Hump swung his legs off the bed and stood up. He
walked over to the table and took a seat where he could
watch Lonnie at the front window.

"You hungry, Lonnie?" he said.

"I sure am."

"Well, I'm sorry that you got to stay there and watch
the trail, but that's just how it is. Me and Etta are going
to sit here and eat. Come on, Etta. Sit down here by me."
He reached over and moved one of the plates beside the
one he was using. Etta sat down. Hump spooned out great
helpings of each dish onto his plate and started to eat. He
looked at Etta who was just sitting there. "Hey," he said.
"What's wrong? Get yourself some food."

"I guess I just ain't hungry," she said.

"Oh, bullshit," said Hump. "A woman like you? You
got to be hungry. Eat up. I figure once I take care of this
fellow what's following me, this damn Slocum, you and
me'll have time for some fun. Just the two of us."

Etta looked at Lonnie standing by the window, and she
looked at the squirrel gun there where Hump had abandoned it propped against the headboard of the bed. It was
about halfway between Hump and the window where

Lonnie was stationed. Hump had put his six-gun on the table beside his plate. "You need some more coffee," she said. "I'll fetch it."

"Say, Lonnie," said Hump. "You got yourself a good woman here. That's just how I like a woman to be. Say, you see anyone there yet?"

Etta got up and went for the coffeepot which was still sitting on the hot stove. She picked up a rag and used it for a potholder. Then she picked up the coffeepot and moved slowly toward Hump.

"I ain't seen nothing coming," said Lonnie. "Nothing at all."

"Well, you just keep your eyes peeled, you hear?"

"Yes, sir," said Lonnie. "I will.

Etta was standing right behind Hump with the pot of boiling coffee in her hand. She looked at Lonnie, hoping that he would pick up on what she was doing fast enough. He ought to be able to get to the squirrel gun fast enough. She knew already what Hump was planning. He was running from someone, and he meant to use their house to kill the man from. Then he would kill Lonnie, and she knew what he planned from there. She had no intention of letting him get away with it. She tipped the pot and poured hot coffee down the back of Hump's shirt.

"Aaaahhhh," Hump screamed. He leaped up from his chair and turned to face her. His six-gun was still lying on the table. Lonnie turned and took it all in. He raced for the squirrel gun. Etta swung the coffeepot with all her strength, bashing it into the side of Hump's head. Hump screamed again, and his scream turned into a growl as he reached for Etta with both hands. Just then Lonnie raised the squirrel gun and fired. The shot tore through Hump's right buttock at an angle. Hump howled, turned to reach for his six-gun, and Lonnie fired again, the shot striking Hump just below the neck, high on the chest. He staggered backward staring at Lonnie with a look of mixed astonishment and hatred. Lonnie fired a third time. The last bullet smacked into Hump's forehead, and Hump fell over hard on his back and lay still.

Etta stared at the body, oozing a pool of blood on her

floor, in disbelief and horror. Lonnie stared only for a moment. Then he put down the gun and rushed to his wife, holding her tight and close in his arms. "It's all right now," he said. "It's over." Etta was shaking. "Oh," she said. "Oh, Lonnie."

Slocum was still easing along the trail when he came to the rise with a house at the top off to the left side. He moved slowly, watching carefully. He could not see Hump's horse, but then, that did not prove anything. The horse could be hidden. The occupants of the house could be dead. Hump could be waiting to gun him from a window or from the front door. He tried to tell if the front door was ajar, but he was still too far away. Perhaps Hump had just rushed on by this house the way he had done the last three. But there was something about the way this house was situated that made it particularly useful for an ambush. Slocum wondered if Hump would have missed that about it. He wouldn't have a better chance.

He was moving slowly on the trail trying to decide how best to approach the house when he heard three shots fired. Quickly he moved his horse to the side of the trail and pulled out his Winchester. Cranking a shell into the chamber, he stared at the house. Anything could have happened in there. The shots sounded as if they came from a small caliber rifle, but that could mean anything. He dismounted and walked toward the house. He heard nothing more. Hump could have murdered the people who lived here. Close enough now for a shot from his Colt, he stopped.

"You in the house," he called out.

The front door opened a crack.

"Who is it?"

"My name's Slocum. I'm trailing a man. A murderer. Is everything all right in there?"

In the house Lonnie looked at his wife. "Did that man say he was going to kill Slocum?" he asked her.

"I think that's what he said."

Lonnie looked back out the door. "Slocum," he yelled. "Come on up, but come slow."

"I'll just fetch my horse," Slocum said. He turned and walked back down the hill to where he had left the Appaloosa and mounted up. He put the Winchester away and started to ride slowly up to the house. When he reached it, Lonnie stepped out the door still holding the squirrel gun.

"I heard some shots," Slocum said.

"If you're really Slocum," said Lonnie, "we got something for you inside."

"Couldn't be someone's in there holding a gun on you or on your wife?" Slocum asked.

"Etta," Lonnie said, "step on out here."

Etta stepped out to stand beside her husband. "There's no one alive in there," she said.

"Who you got inside?" Slocum asked.

"Called himself Hump," Lonnie said.

"By God," said Slocum, "that's who I'm after. Can I get down?"

"Come ahead," said Lonnie, still holding the squirrel gun.

Slocum swung down and walked slowly toward the house. He hesitated a moment at the door.

"Go ahead," Lonnie said.

Slocum stepped inside and saw the body. He walked around the table to get a better look. It was Hump Beamer all right. The last of the Beamers.

21

Lonnie and Etta were both nervous. Neither one had ever killed a man before. They told Slocum in detail just what had happened. Their tale told him that he had been right. Hump Beamer had planned to ambush him from the small house, and his plans had been thwarted by the quick thinking of Etta. When they had finished with the story, Slocum said, "You all did just the right thing. He'd have killed me first, then Lonnie, and then—Well, you did just right. That was a smart and a brave thing you did, ma'am."

"But what do we do now?" Etta said. "We have a dead man right here in our house. Won't there have to be a trial or an inquest or something? We have to tell someone what happened here."

"You told me," said Slocum. "That's enough. I was after him legal. I'll take him out of here, and I'll explain everything to the sheriff when I get back."

"Thanks," said Lonnie.

Slocum lugged the remains of Hump Beamer outside and loaded them on Hump's last stolen horse. Then he went back inside. There was a big pool of blood on the floor where Hump had fallen. Slocum did not think that Etta would be up to cleaning the mess, and he wasn't sure about Lonnie either. He asked Etta for a pail of soapy water and a brush or a rag. Then he swabbed the deck. He was about to leave when they invited him to stay for a meal. Etta cleaned the table of the mess that Hump had left, and soon they all sat down to eat. At last there was no more to be done, and Slocum had a long ride back to Tipton's place or to Breakneck, either way he figured it. He said his good-byes and left, riding his Appaloosa and leading the extra horse with the foul load.

Riding along the lonely trail, Slocum considered the irony of the whole situation. He had gone after Hump almost desperate, fully determined to find the man and kill him, only to find his body, killed by someone else. Hump had been killed by two innocents. Slocum could not imagine anyone less likely to have done in the horrible murderer than Lonnie and Etta. Along the way, he decided that the carcass was going to get too rank to carry all the way back. He stopped by the side of the road, scooped out a shallow grave and rolled the wretched thing in. Then he threw the dirt back in, mounted up, and moved on. He found the horse of the man he had promised to bring it back to and took it along. The owner was so grateful that he provided Slocum with another meal. Along the way, he stopped everywhere there were survivors and told them what had happened. He returned what property he could.

Carl Tipton had spent another night in Breakneck. He had taken six ranch hands into town with him, and they all knew why he had wanted to spend the night. No one said anything about it though. They had just made the best they could of the situation, enjoying a night in town at the boss's expense. It was early morning, and they were on their way back to the ranch. They had gone about half the distance and were rounding a sharp curve in the road when a rifle shot sounded, shattering the morning silence. The cowhands all fought to control their frightened horses. Carl Tipton jerked in the saddle. He too fought with his mount but only feebly. When the cowhands got their horses back under control, Charlie Hope noticed that his boss was having trouble. He rode up to steady the horse, and he saw the bloodstain on Carl's chest.

"Hey," he said, "the boss's been hit."

He reached over to steady Tipton in the saddle.

"Hold on, Boss," he said. "We'll get you home."

Tipton stared at Charlie with wide eyes that suddenly went blank. He went limp and sagged in the saddle. Charlie had difficulty holding him up.

"Someone help me here," he said.

Two cowhands dismounted and took Tipton to lower him to the ground. One of them leaned over him for a moment. He looked up at the others with a shocked expression on his face. "He's dead," he said.

"Where'd the shot come from?" asked Charlie Hope.

"I'd say up yonder," said one of the hands, pointing almost dead ahead.

"You two stay with the boss," said Charlie. "The rest of you come with me."

The two cowboys that had lowered the body stayed there, and Charlie Hope and the other four rode hard toward the place they supposed the shots had come from. They did not see anyone riding away. They rode around for a while until they discovered the place from which the shots had been fired. One of them picked up a lone shell. It was still hot. They looked around some more but never found a trail. At last they rode back to where the two hands waited with the body of Carl Tipton.

"We found a shell," said Charlie. "Nothing else. Let's get on back to the ranch. No use putting this thing off."

Slocum rode first into Breakneck to the rooming house where the sheriff was laid up. He reported the activities all along the way and the final outcome to Seth Willis. Willis was doing much better by this time. He was dressed and sitting up in a chair. When Slocum went in to his room, he was drinking a cup of coffee. He called for another for Slocum. When Slocum had finished his story, Seth took another sip of coffee and put the cup down on the small table that stood beside his chair.

"Well," he said, "I reckon that's the end of it. Maybe now things will get back to normal around here."

"Yeah," Slocum said. "I guess I'll be riding on."

"You ain't staying around?"

"Got no reason to," Slocum said.

"You got no reason to leave either," said the sheriff.

Slocum thought about his near entanglement with both Jamie and with Harmony. He thought about the fact that he knew about Carl Tipton's sordid affair in town while he had a perfectly nice wife out at his ranch.

"Before I got hooked up with ole Tipton," he said, "I was just passing through."

"Well," Seth said, "if you should change your mind, most everyone around would be just tickled to have you stay."

"Thanks," Slocum said. "I reckon I'll be getting back out to the ranch to tell ole Carl what's happened. He'll be pleased to know that he can rove free and easy again."

"Yeah," Seth said. "I know he will."

Slocum went outside and was about to mount his Appaloosa when he saw Randy Self and Charlie Hope come riding into town. When they saw him, they rode directly over to where the horse was tied up. They both dismounted.

"Howdy, boys," Slocum said.

"Slocum," said Randy. "Man, I'm glad you're back."

"Well," Slocum said, "it's all over."

"I reckon so," said Randy. "The damn Beamers got Carl."

"What are you talking about?" Slocum said. "The last Beamer is dead."

"Then I reckon you got him a little late," Randy said.

"They got Carl from an ambush," said Charlie. "I was riding along with him when it happened. We couldn't pick up no trail. All we got was this shell casing."

He pulled the spent shell out of his shirt pocket and handed it to Slocum. Slocum turned it over in his palm and studied it.

"Boys," he said, "it couldn't have been a Beamer. There was just the one left, and I been on his trail all this time. He'd dead. I buried the body. It had to have been someone else."

"That don't make sense," said Charlie.

"If it wasn't the Beamers—"

"It wasn't," Slocum said. "I'm telling you."

"Then who the hell could it have been?" Randy finished.

Slocum studied the shell some more.

"I'd call this a forty caliber," he said. "It wasn't shot from no Winchester. Likely not from a Henry. My guess would be a Sharps buffalo gun."

"I ain't seen one of them around here," Randy said. "Not for a while."

"Keep your eyes open," said Slocum. "What are you boys doing here in town? I was just about to head out to the ranch to tell ole Carl what's happened. I reckon I'll tell the ladies now."

"We come in to tell Seth about the boss," said Randy. "This is the first we've been to town since it happened."

"And then?"

"I guess we'll go back out to the ranch."

"Go on in and tell him," Slocum said, "and then I'll ride back out there with you."

Charlie and Randy went in to see the sheriff, and Slocum pulled a cigar out of his pocket and lit it. He had been thinking that his job was over and that he would head on out of town. But now someone unknown had murdered old Carl Tipton. Technically, Slocum guessed, his job was over. He had hired on to protect old Carl from the Beamers, and now the Beamers were all dead, but then so was old Carl. Slocum figured that the job he had been hired to do included many surprises like this. And even though his boss was now dead, his job wasn't really over until he had found the killer or killers and brought them to justice, whichever kind of justice happened to work out.

Charlie and Randy came back out, and the three of them mounted up. They rode toward the ranch for a while in silence. At last, Slocum broke the spell. "How did ole Seth take the news?" he asked. "They seemed to me like they was pretty good friends."

"Yeah," Randy said. "They went back a few years. He took it kind of hard, I'd say."

"Yeah," Charlie agreed. "Kind of hard. He figured, like you, that with the last of the Beamers done in, ole Carl would be safe."

"We tried to figure who it might be," said Randy. "The boss just didn't have any enemies around here. Except for the Beamers, of course. It don't make any sense."

"No sense at all," said Charlie.

Slocum had not been around long enough to add anything to that.

"Oh, yeah," said Randy. "Seth said that as sheriff he can officiate at the reading of the will. He said that he knowed that Mr. Tipton left a will and had it filed all proper. Seth set the day for the reading of it in two days from today at 1:00 in the afternoon. Said he didn't want to rush the ladies into town. Course, it's just a formality. The ranch belongs to Mrs. Tipton now. I guess we'll all of us stay on and run it for her as long as she wants us to."

"That's good," Slocum said.

Back at the ranch, Slocum found both women in a solemn mood. They were over the initial shock of the killing. The crying time was past. Myrtle was going about her household duties with a long face, and Jamie was doing what she could to help. Like everyone else, they had assumed that the dirty deed had been done by a Beamer, but when Slocum told them the tale of the fate of the last Beamer, they, like everyone else, had gone into deep thought.

"Who could it have been?" said Myrtle.

"It's crazy," Jamie said.

"I mean to find out," Slocum told them. "I feel like I let him down. He hired me to protect him."

"Daddy hired you to protect him from the Beamers," Jamie said. "You did that. You did an admirable job of it, and at the time he was killed, you were on the trail of the last of them. He might even have already been dead from the way you tell it. You can't blame yourself, Slocum."

"Slocum," said Myrtle, "you did your job. We're grateful for it. If you want to move on, no one here will think any the less of you. On the other hand, we'd love for you to stay. You'll have a job here as long as we're around."

"Thank you, ma'am," Slocum said. "I think that I'll

just remove myself from the payroll though. I'll pack up my things and move into town. But I'll be staying around. I mean to find out who done this thing."

"You don't have to move out," said Jamie. "You can—"

"I'll be looking for some things," he said. "I'll see more in town."

"Whatever you think is best," Myrtle said. "Slocum, I'm glad you're staying on. I hope you find out who did it. I hope you find out real soon."

Slocum packed up his few belongings and strapped them in a bedroll behind his saddle. He said his good-byes to Randy and to Charlie and a few more of the boys, and then he rode back into Breakneck. He was hungry, so he went by Harmony's place for a meal and some coffee. She was busy when he got up to leave, so he just put his cash on the counter and walked out. He took the Appaloosa to the stable and put him up for the night with instructions to the man there to feed him well and take good care of him. Then he walked down the street toward the Hogneck. All along the way, he looked at the rifles in the saddle boots on horses. When he saw a man carrying a rifle, he took note of it. Everything he saw was .45 caliber.

He went inside the Hogneck and paid the man for a room upstairs. He pocketed the key and took his bedroll up and tossed it on the bed. Then he went back out, locking the door behind himself. He went back into the saloon and bought a bottle of good bourbon whiskey. He took the bottle and a glass over to a table and sat down. He looked over the crowd thinking that there could be a murderer among them. He poured a drink and downed it at once. He still had an unpleasant feeling, a bad taste in his mouth. He thought that he wrapped up a job, only to find that someone had come up and blindsided him, and he had no idea who that someone might be.

He poured another drink, and this time he sipped it. He figured it was going to take several of these, hell, maybe the whole damn bottle, to get that taste out of his mouth. He then realized that he was angry, really angry

at whoever it was who had killed Carl Tipton. He felt like
there had been a major conspiracy involving the Beamers
to get him off the track. Of course, he knew that had not
been the case. The Beamers would not have been involved. They wouldn't have gotten themselves all killed
just to help someone else along. Still, the feeling was
there. Someone had damn sure taken advantage of Slocum's preoccupation with the Beamers to murder ole Carl.
He just couldn't figure out who it might be.

He had to try to think like a lawman and figure out
who Carl's death would benefit. He couldn't think of anyone other than Carl's brother. What was his name? Arnie.
That was it. Arnie Tipton. But then what the hell good
would Carl's death do Arnie? Carl was Arnie's saviour.
Arnie ran a sorry-assed little ranch, if you could even call
what he did running it, and whenever he got himself into
a financial bind, he went crying to his big brother. And
from what it looked like, Carl always bailed him out. No,
it didn't make sense at all to look in Arnie's direction.
There had to be someone else. Slocum decided that first
thing in the morning he would have another talk with
Seth. Maybe Carl played poker, and maybe he had gotten
someone mad at him in a game somehow or other. Such
things happened. Maybe there had been some cattle deal
or something like that. Seth should be able to fill him in
on some of these things. There had to be a way to figure
it all out.

22

Slocum hung loose around Breakneck for the next two days. He did have that long talk with Seth Willis, but he learned absolutely nothing from it. The rest of his time was spent in eyeballing every person he saw in town and in watching for any suspicious Sharps rifles. He went to the hardware store and showed the man the empty shell casing. He asked him if he had sold any of those to anyone lately. The man took it and rolled it around in his hand.

"Forty caliber," he said.

"Yeah. I know."

"Likely a Sharps."

"That's what I figured."

"I sold some to someone a while back," the man said. "Can't recall just who it was bought them. It might could have been old Yancey Jones. Yeah. I believe it was old Yancey. Say, I heard someone murdered the crazy old coot here recently. You know anything about that?"

"No," Slocum said, and he left the store. If old Yancey had owned a Sharps, it could be that the Beamers stole it when they killed him, but that didn't get Slocum anywhere. All of the Beamers but Hump had been killed long before Tipton was murdered, and Slocum was right on Hump's trail at the time. That didn't help either. He felt like he was walking on a dead-end road and there was no place to turn off. There was an answer out there somewhere, though, and he meant to find it. He was about to walk into Harmony's place when he realized that it was about time for the reading of the will. He changed directions and headed for the sheriff's office. Along the way he saw Seth Willis, moving slowly with the help of a walking stick, but moving along on his own. He was glad to see Seth up and around, and he hurried along to meet him and to walk with him.

"Say," Slocum said, "you look to me like you're doing pretty well there."

"I'm getting along," said Willis. "You coming by for the reading of the will?"

"Yes, I am. Where are we going?"

"My office," said Willis.

The walked the rest of the way to the office together, and when they got close they could see a wagon parked in front. Sure enough, when they went inside, they found the two Tipton women waiting in the office with Randy Self and Charlie Hope. Everyone said hello to everyone else. Then they each found a chair while the sheriff moved on around behind his desk and sat down, slowly and with a groan. He reached inside his vest and took a copy of the will out of his pocket. He laid it down on the desk and carefully smoothed it out.

"Mrs. Tipton," he said, "this here is the copy of the last will and testament that Carl put on file with the county. Do you have another copy, one of your own that he left with you?"

"Yes," said Myrtle. "I do."

She stood up and walked to the desk and handed Seth her copy of the will. As she moved back to her chair, Seth laid out the second copy right by the side of the first and studied them together, comparing the handwriting and the wording. Finally he looked up at the small crowd gathered there in his office.

"They appear to be identical," he said. Then he commenced to read from one copy out loud. There wasn't much to it. It was as everyone had expected. The ranch and everything on it as well as all the money in the bank was left to Myrtle, and in the event that anything happened to Myrtle, it went to Jamie. Slocum felt guilty that he was even a little disappointed. But he was. He had cherished a slight and secret hope that the will would reveal something that would help him find the killer. Finished with the reading, Seth folded the papers up, put the one back in his pocket and held the other out toward Myrtle, who stood up to retrieve it. "That just about does it," he said. "There shouldn't be any trouble. Myrtle, I'm sure sorry about what happened, but it looks like Carl left you well taken care of. If there's anything I can help you with, let me know. Will you, please?"

"Thank you, Seth, I will," Myrtle said. Turning to Randy, she said, "Let's go home."

The whole Tipton crew got up and walked out to the waiting wagon. Randy and Charlie helped the women up, and Randy got in to drive. Charlie mounted a horse and rode along beside them. Slocum stayed behind in the sheriff's office, sitting quietly in his chair.

"What is it, Slocum?" Seth asked.

"Nothing," said Slocum. "I was just hoping that the will might tell me something."

"And?"

"It didn't. Not a damn thing."

"Maybe something'll turn up."

"Well, there's been nothing so far," Slocum said. "A Sharps rifle. That's all. I think it was a Sharps."

"Yeah."

"Sheriff," Slocum said, "what could I be missing? Could it be that the Beamers had a friend or an ally of some kind? Another relative hanging around somewhere that we're unaware of?"

"No one that I know about, Slocum. Course, anything's possible."

"If it is someone connected with the Beamers, then he'll be after me, too. I been pretty conspicuous around town here the last couple of days. Maybe I'll take some time to ride out by myself. See if I can smoke someone out."

"You do that, you be careful," Willis said.

"Don't worry about that. I'm not looking to get myself killed, just to catch a skunk."

By that time, Seth Willis was pretty well worn out. It had been the first day he had gotten up and out by himself. Slocum walked with him back to the boardinghouse and saw him up to his room. Then he went back outside and stood on the sidewalk for a moment. He let his mind wander, and suddenly it lit on something he supposed he had put out of his mind for some reason. It lit on Bonita. Not that he suspected Bonita, but Bonita might know something. In a relationship like that one, sometimes a man told all kinds of things to the gal that he kept to himself otherwise. Slocum walked back to the Hogneck. Goosey said that Bonita was still upstairs, likely still asleep.

"What's her room number?" Slocum asked.

"I told you," Goosey said, "she's most likely asleep. She'll be down here later on in the day. You can come back then and—"

Slocum reached across the bar and grabbed Goosey by the shirtfront pulling him halfway over. "All I asked you for was the room number," he said.

"Six," said Goosey.

Slocum shoved Goosey away and turned to walk to the stairs. He went upstairs and found number six. He knocked on the door and got no immediate reaction, so he knocked again louder.

"Who is it?" came a weak voice from inside.

"It's Slocum. I want to talk to you."

He was about to knock a third time when the door was opened and Bonita peered out. She looked much worse than normal without her makeup and with her hair mussed from sleeping. Her eyes were bleary from lack of sleep, and she squinted through them at Slocum.

"What do you want?" she said.

"Can I come in?"

Bonita stepped back, and Slocum walked in. He shut the door. Bonita walked back to the bed and sat on the edge looking at Slocum. She was still not quite awake.

"What do you want?" she asked him again.

"I want to talk about Carl Tipton."

"What makes you think I know anything about Carl?" she said.

"Come on," said Slocum. "You know a whole lot about most everyone around here. And I suspect you know even more about Carl than about most. It ain't no secret about you and him. Unless maybe from Myrtle."

"All right. So what?"

"Look. I'm not here to judge you or to cause any trouble. You know that Carl was murdered?"

For the first time the expression on her face softened, and for a moment, Slocum was afraid that she would start crying. "I know," she said. "I heard."

"All I'm trying to do is find out who did it. The Beamers were all dead when it happened. It had to be someone else. Can you think of anyone else who had a reason to kill Carl? Anyone at all."

She shook her head. "No," she said. "I can't help you."

"What about his brother?"

"Arnie?" Bonita laughed. "Arnie couldn't exist without Carl. I don't know what'll happen to him now. I don't think that Myrtle will support him the way Carl did."

"So Arnie's a big loser in this deal," Slocum said.

"He sure is. Oh, he'll come around the ranch and beg Myrtle to help him out for Carl's sake, but I think she'll just turn him out. He'll wind up selling his pitiful little ranch, spending all the money, and then—who knows what?"

"Did Carl ever say anything to you about anyone who—"

"Believe me, Slocum, if I knew anything, I'd tell you. I—liked Carl. I want to see you get the son of a bitch that killed him. I'd like to be there to watch. But I just don't know anything that will help you."

Slocum walked to the door and put a hand on the knob. "Okay," he said. "Thanks. If anything should come to you, let me know. All right?"

"Sure," she said.

Slocum opened the door and was stepping out into the hallway when Bonita stopped him. "Slocum," she said.

He turned back to face her.

"Lots of folks might say that I had the best motive going. I knew that he'd never leave Myrtle for me, and you know what they say about a woman scorned."

On his way down the stairs, Slocum thought about what Bonita had said about Arnie. He hated to turn loose of Arnie as a suspect. He did not like Arnie. But it sure made sense what Bonita had said. Arnie was a sponge on Carl, and without Carl, he had nothing. He guessed he'd have to quit thinking about Arnie.

Slocum rode out to the Tipton ranch that afternoon. No one bothered him along the way, but as he was approaching the main gate he saw Arnie Tipton ride away. He stopped and watched Arnie for a moment. Then he rode on in. Jamie came out onto the porch and met him.

"Howdy, Slocum," she said. "I been missing you around here."

"Thanks," he said. He climbed down off his horse and walked up onto the porch. "Mind if I have a seat?"

"Please do."

He sat down, and so did she. "So," she said. "What's brings you way out here?"

"I just thought I needed to get out of town for a while. Take a little ride. Couldn't think of a better place, so here I am."

"I know what you mean," she said. "Have you made any progress?"

"No. I've talked to Seth and to—well, a bunch of folks, but I haven't learned a damn thing."

"Was one of that bunch of folks a gal named Bonita?"

Slocum looked at Jamie, his brow wrinkled.

"Oh, don't worry," she said, "I know all about Bonita."

"Does your mother—"

"No. She doesn't."

"Okay. Yeah. I talked to her."

"Nothing?"

"Nothing. Say, was that your Uncle Arnie I saw riding away from here?"

"Yeah. He just called to say his condolences."

"Nothing else?"

"If you mean did he ask for money, no, he didn't."

"Have you had any more thoughts on who it might

have been?" Slocum asked her. "You or your mother?"

Jamie looked down at the boards of the porch and slowly shook her head. "No," she said. "Not a thought. I've tried and tried. I can't come up with anything. It still just doesn't make any sense, Slocum. It doesn't make any sense."

Slocum was still on that dead-end road. He had no idea where to turn or where to look or what kind of questions to ask or who to ask the questions of. He wrapped up the conversation as quickly and smoothly as he could and rode back to town. Again, he had no trouble. If anyone was watching him, the bastard had decided to wait a bit before making his move. But Slocum had given him a perfect chance and a perfect time. He had been clear and open about riding out of town, and he had gone out alone. If it was a cohort of the Beamers, then why didn't the son of a bitch make a try for him? He made it back to Breakneck after dark, and he thought about stopping by to see Harmony. Her place was already closed. He decided to skip it. He took his horse back to the stable and walked the distance to the Hogneck.

Inside he ordered some whiskey and sat down at a table with bottle and glass. He looked at everyone in the place with suspicion. He was damn sure in the mood to do some killing, but he did not know who he should kill.

Then Seth Willis came walking in with his cane. He saw Slocum and headed for the table, stopping by the bar for a glass. At the table he held out the empty glass.

"Buy me a drink?" he asked.

"Or two," said Slocum. "Sit down."

Willis pulled out a chair and sat down. He was still moving slowly and carefully, and he moaned when the weight was lifted from his legs. Slocum poured him a drink and shoved the glass back over toward him. Willis lifted it.

"Thanks," he said. He took a long drink. "Ahh. That's the first whiskey I've had since I got shot."

"You better watch yourself then," Slocum said. "You don't want to get staggering drunk the shape you're in."

"I'll have those two like you said, and then I'll quit. I

still have to get myself back over to the rooming house. Just thought it was about time."

"I'd say so."

"How'd your day go?"

"Hell," said Slocum, "I rode out to the Tipton spread. No one bothered me either way. I seen ole Arnie riding away just as I come up, and then I went on in and talked to Jamie for a spell. She didn't have nothing new to add. I just wasted the day. That's all."

"The only thing I can think of to say, Slocum, is that if it was a Beamer partner that done the killing, like you said before, he'll be coming after you, too. Keep giving him chances, he'll show himself."

23

For the next several days, Slocum rode out again, each time he rode alone. He rode in different directions. No one followed him that he could tell. No one shot at him. No one bothered him at all. He was ready to give up. The murder of old Carl Tipton would just have to remain a mystery. He wanted to find the killer and even the score for Tipton, but he had no intention of making this his life's work. He thought that he would give it a couple of days more. Then he would just ride out and put it all behind him. He'd had a morning ride, gotten himself a meal at Harmony's place, and was on his way back to the Hogneck for a drink. After that, he thought, he would just to go to bed and take a nice, long afternoon nap. As he was walking along the sidewalk, he was hailed by Seth Willis. He stopped and turned around.

"Howdy, Sheriff," he said. "What's up?"

"Can you come over to the office with me?" Seth said. "Sure."

Slocum walked with Willis to the sheriff's office. Along the way he noticed how much better the sheriff was doing. He was no longer even carrying his walking stick with him.

"You're sure making good progress," he said.

"I guess so," said Seth. "It seems slow to me, but everyone's telling me that."

They reached the office and Willis opened the door and stepped aside. Slocum walked in first. He waited for the

sheriff to come in and shut the door, then get around behind his big desk and sit down.

"Pull up a chair, Slocum," said the sheriff.

Slocum dragged a chair up to the desk to sit across
from Seth.

"I had an interesting visit from ole Arnie," Seth said,
opening his desk drawer to withdraw a couple of papers.

"Arnie Tipton?" said Slocum.

"The one and only. He brought me this paper." Seth
tossed one of the papers across the desk to Slocum. Slocum picked it up and studied it. It was headed, "Last Will
and Testament of Carl Tipton." He looked up at the sheriff.

"Is this the same document you read to the family?"
Slocum asked.

"It's almost identical to it," said Seth, "but read on
down through it. You'll see where it differs from the other
one."

Slocum read. Suddenly he looked up at Seth. "This one
here says that the ranch all goes to Arnie," he said.

"That's what it says. It also says that it takes the place
of any former will, and it's dated real recent. When Arnie
brought it in, he said that Carl had written it out at his
place. He said that Carl was worried that Myrtle wouldn't
be able to hold the ranch together. He thought that Arnie
had ought to do it, if he would promise to take care of
Myrtle and Jamie, and Arnie promised that he would do
that."

Slocum looked back at the document. "What does it
say about the money in the bank?"

"It goes to Arnie."

"All of it?"

"Every damn cent. According to Arnie, Carl was worried that Myrtle and Jamie might spend it all foolishly.
He thought that it would be better if Arnie had control
over the funds."

"Well, did Carl write this?"

"I ain't no expert, Slocum," said Seth, "but I compared
the handwriting on this one to the handwriting on the
other one, and they sure do look the same to me."

"I can't believe that ole Carl would do this to his own wife and daughter," said Slocum. "He sure wasn't no model husband, but I still can't believe this."

Seth gave a shrug. "All I'm doing is just showing you what he brought me," he said.

"Has Myrtle seen this yet?"

"Not yet."

"Do you feel up to a ride?"

"I sure do."

"Let's go out there," said Slocum.

In another minute both men were up and on their way out the door. They made the ride out to the Tipton spread without much talk. When they arrived at the ranch, they found the hands all working and the two women in the house. Myrtle invited them in and poured them coffee. They sat at the big dining table, and Seth brought out the document and showed it to Myrtle. She gasped when she read it.

"Where did you get this?" she asked.

"Arnie brought it by the office," Seth said.

"I can't believe it."

"Does it look like Carl's writing to you?" Slocum asked.

"It does," said Myrtle, "but I still can't believe it."

"Study it real careful, Myrtle, if you will," said Seth. "The handwriting, I mean."

Myrtle poured over the document some more. At last she dropped the paper onto the table and leaned back in her chair shaking her head.

"It looks like Carl's writing," she said. "How could he do this to me?"

Seth told Myrtle what Arnie had said that Carl had told him about his reasons for writing a new will.

"That's nonsense," Myrtle said. "Carl would never have said that. I'm a better businessman than Carl ever was, and he knew it. He admitted it. He always consulted me on business matters, and what's more, he would never have trusted Arnie with anything important. Why, Arnie's a dodo when it comes to anything about money, and Carl knew that, too."

"That's about what I thought," said Slocum.

"Well," said Seth, "me, too, but I got to consider this thing here. I told Arnie to give me a couple of days to study on this. I told him if we determined that the will was genuine, we'd have to get a judge in here as soon as possible to make a determination. He's supposed to come back in to my office day after tomorrow to see what I've got to say about it."

"Day after tomorrow?" said Slocum.

"That's right."

"Let's just sit on this thing till then, Seth," Slocum said. "When Arnie comes back in to see you, put him off somehow. Give me a little time to do some nosing around."

"You can't do your nosing before then?"

"Just trust me on this," Slocum said.

"What are you going to do? What are you looking for?"

"I don't think you want to know."

Slocum passed the rest of that day and all of the next like a man with no worries. He did not bother riding out again. He ate his meals at Harmony's place, drank in the Hogneck, and slept in his rented room there. He passed a little time with Harmony and a little with Seth Willis. He even visited some with Bonita in the saloon. On the morning of the day Arnie was scheduled to show up back at the sheriff's office, Slocum was up and out early. He rode out toward Arnie Tipton's wretched ranch, and he hid beside the road and waited. He waited until he saw Arnie come riding out, move onto the road and head for town. It was a good two hours ride into town. Slocum knew that he had plenty of time. He waited for Arnie to get some distance away, and then he rode on in to Arnie's house. He dismounted in front and walked up to the door. He was not really surprised to find it unlocked. He walked in and looked around.

The place was a mess. It stank from unwashed dishes, unwashed clothes, and leftover food. There were empty bottles all over the place. It took a couple of minutes, but

Slocum spotted the Sharps rifle propped up in a corner of the room. He walked over and picked it up. It was enough for him, but it would not be enough for the sheriff or for a jury. He knew that. He walked around looking under things, looking in corners, looking on the messy floor. Then he saw a stack of papers on a corner of the table. The table was a mess of dishes and other things. He walked over to thumb through the pages, and he found several sheets covered with the signature, "Carl Tipton." He studied the pages carefully. The signature gradually changed. Then he found some sheets that were copies of the same will Arnie had taken to Seth's office. The writing changed on those as well from one copy to the next. He did not have any samples of Carl Tipton's writing to compare to these, but he surmised that Arnie had been practicing the handwriting before writing the final copy of the forged will.

Slocum stuffed the papers into his shirt and picked up the Sharps rifle. He went outside, mounted his Appaloosa and rode fast to the Carl Tipton ranch. Jamie was on the porch when he rode up to the big house.

"Jamie," he called out, "get your mother. Get a couple of the boys to drive you two into town to the sheriff's office. I ain't got time to explain it right now. I got to get there before Arnie leaves."

"But—"

Slocum did not wait for an answer. He turned his horse and rode off toward town. He could not afford to ride the Appaloosa hard all the way, so he moved along at a fast pace for a little while and then slowed down for a space before speeding up again. When at last he arrived at Seth Willis's office, he was pleased to see that Arnie's horse was still tied up out front. He dismounted, tied his Appaloosa, took the Sharps rifle, and went inside. Arnie was seated across the desk from Seth.

"I don't see what the problem is here," Arnie was saying as Slocum walked in. He turned his head to look at Slocum, and then he shut up.

"There's no problem, Arnie," said Willis. "These things just take time. That's all. Whenever you're contesting a will, there's lots of legal issues to consider."

Arnie looked over at Slocum.

"Don't mind me," Slocum said.

"I think we was having a private conversation," said Arnie.

"Slocum knows all about this," Seth said. "No need to try to keep the conversation from him."

"It ain't none of his damn business. He was just a hired hand of Carl's, and Carl's dead now. I ain't going to talk anymore if he's here."

"Suit yourself," Seth said.

Arnie stood up. "I'll come back when you ain't got unwanted company," he said.

"You just sit back down, Arnie," said Slocum.

"What?"

"You heard me."

"I don't have to do what you say."

Slocum raised up the Sharps and tossed it at Arnie, who caught it just in time to keep it from smashing into his chest.

"What's this?" he said.

"Don't you recognize it?" Slocum said.

"Well, no, I, well, yes. It looks like my gun."

"I reckon it is," Slocum said. "I got it out of your house."

"You been in my house? Sheriff, I want this son of a bitch arrested for trespassing, and for stealing my gun."

"It don't look stole to me," said Seth. "You're holding it, ain't you?"

"But you heard what he said."

"That's a forty caliber, ain't it?" Slocum said. "You see many of those old Sharps rifles around here, Seth?"

"Hardly ever see one."

Slocum reached into his shirt pocket and pulled out the forty caliber shell that had been found at the scene of Carl Tipton's murder. He tossed it to Seth.

"You recall that the boys that was riding with Carl found this shell at the scene," he said. "When they picked it up, it was still hot."

"I remember," Seth said.

"It looks to be forty caliber," said Slocum.

"That don't mean nothing," said Arnie. "There's lots of forty caliber guns around."

Seth stood up and held a hand out toward Arnie. "Let me see yours," he said.

"What for?"

"Let me see it."

Arnie handed the rifle to Seth, and Seth opened it up and place the spent shell in the chamber. "It sure enough fits," he said.

"So would any forty caliber shell."

"You're right," Seth said. "But it is a bit suspicious."

"A bit suspicious don't mean a damn thing," Arnie said. "Give me back my gun. I'm getting out of here."

Slocum heard the sound of a wagon in the street, and he stepped over to look out the window. Randy Self had just driven Myrtle and Jamie up.

"Not so fast," he said to Arnie. "There's someone coming in who might want to hear some of this."

"I don't care about that," Arnie said.

"Sit down, Arnie," said Seth.

The door opened and the two Tipton ladies stepped in. They looked from Arnie to Slocum and then to Seth.

"Come on in, ladies," Seth said.

They walked in closer. Myrtle looked at Slocum. "What's this all about?" she said.

Slocum reached into his shirt and withdrew the stack of papers he had taken from Arnie's house. He stepped over close to the desk and laid them on it. Arnie's eyes opened wide.

"Give those to me," he said.

"How come?" Slocum said.

"You had no right to go into my house and get that stuff."

"Then you admit it's yours?" Slocum said.

"Wait. No. I don't know what the hell you're talking about."

Myrtle moved to the desk and picked up the stack of papers. She went through several of the sheets, more astonished the more she looked. She dropped them back on the desk and looked at Slocum.

"You found these at Arnie's house?" she said.

"Yes, ma'am," said Slocum. "Along with his forty caliber rifle there."

Jamie moved toward Arnie as if she would scratch out his eyes, but Slocum grabbed her and restrained her. "You," she said, staring hard at Arnie. "You killed my father. You son of a bitch. Your own brother. Just to get his ranch."

"No. I didn't. You got to believe me. I didn't."

Seth picked up the stack of papers and studied it over. "It's pretty clear that we have evidence here of you practicing on Carl's writing in order to forge a new will. That along with the rifle ought to get you convicted of murder."

"No," said Arnie. "I didn't—"

Slocum was still holding Jamie. He could feel when the Colt was lifted from the holster at his side, but he did not have time to react. He could only look to his right as Myrtle lifted the revolver, as she aimed it at Arnie's chest, as she cocked the hammer and pulled the trigger. He looked toward Arnie just as the bullet smashed into his chest, watched as Arnie crumpled up on the floor in front of the sheriff's desk and then lay there, still and dead. Jamie looked at her mother, as Slocum turned her loose.

"Mother," she said.

Myrtle handed the Colt to Slocum. He put it away. Then Myrtle walked toward Seth.

"You can go on ahead and arrest me," she said. "I won't give you no trouble."

"No, ma'am," Seth said. "I ain't going to arrest you. I'll fill out a report that will make everything look legitimate. You and Jamie can just go on back home now. I'll take care of it all."

Watch for

SLOCUM AND THE ORPHAN EXPRESS

303rd novel in the exciting SLOCUM series
from Jove

Coming in May!

JAKE LOGAN
TODAY'S HOTTEST ACTION WESTERN!